praise for Anthony Valerio~

"He's just crazy enough. He knows his craft. He gets in, tells his story and gets out. It's what good writing should be."-- **Shel Silverstein**

"Anthony Valerio's version of life in Brooklyn is dream-like, sometimes fantastical, yet all the more real to us, made so by a daring style and a seeming love for his characters." --**The Baltimore Sun**

"The book has zest, high humor, madness, detached reflection, and pathos." **--Los Angeles Times**

"A wonderful read."**--Larry King,** *USA Today*

"Anthony Valerio really knows both his history and his subject very well. No less important is the fact that he is a first-rate writer who can really tell a good story." – **Bestsellers**

Library of Congress Control Number: 2013943632
ISBN 10: 0-9772824-9-X

Also by Anthony Valerio~

The MEDITERRANEAN RUNS THROUGH BROOKLYN

BART: *a Life of A. Bartlett Giamatti*

THE LITTLE SAILOR, *a Romantic Thriller*

ANITA GARIBALDI, a Biography

TONI CADE BAMBARA'S ONE SICILIAN NIGHT, *a Memoir*

JOHN DANTE'S INFERNO, *a Playboy's Life*

to Daisy, Always

Easy Time

Sometimes she stops by on a whim, after a night out with friends, an afternoon with the monkeys at the Bronx Zoo. She believes her visits are impromptu, a surprise, but she reveals her next day's itinerary during her evening phone call and so I'm able to track the hours, know approximately when she's on her way home. I stay home on the chance that the desire suddenly arises in her to see me.

One Saturday night she said, "Last Thursday after teaching I passed your door and almost came in."

I said, "What was your thinking, your precise thinking that resulted in your continuing on your way?" and from then on she sometimes stops by after teaching, around five thirty, and I'm home.

Her first surprise visit occurred two days after our first night alone, a Saturday. We had kissed the night away. I got up from our dinner table to get the pasta and on the way back leaned down to kiss the back of her head. Before my lips touched strands of her red hair, she turned slowly, closing her eyes, projecting her desire into the infinite darkness from the end of which my desire raced toward hers. Her lips parted. Her lips are always parted due to a protuberance of her upper teeth. She parts her lips even more for a kiss. Kissing softly, I held out my hand and guided her to her feet as though we were about to dance. Arms around waists, we glided to the yellow club chair. I sat down and she sat on my lap. She fit like a little girl, her thin, slightly bowed legs across mine, her shoes dangling from her small toes, lavish earrings knocked by my arms, my kisses, to the red floor. She pulled away to catch her breath. "You're going to complicate my life," she sighed.

"I'm not going to let you leave here," I said.

"Don't tell me that again."

"I'm not going to let you leave here."

Around eleven o'clock, she said, "I have to go now."

I grasped her ankle where her white ankle sock fringed with lace meets her skin.

We left together as though our destination were the same. I waited outside while she bought the Sunday papers. I took them from her so she would feel light, free, then I took her arm. She pulled it away. "Not on this block," she said. "Not in this neighborhood."

We detoured west toward the river, north on Greenwich Street which runs parallel to Hudson Street, where we could have walked arm in arm if she felt free. On Bethune Street there is a huge planter with a thick cement lip. We sat on it and had a last smoke, silent in the open air. I got up first to guide her to our last corner. She trailed after me, stopped. "Hey, come back here!" she called.

I went back to her, she cupped my chin and carried my lips to hers, and we closed our eyes.

"See you soon," she said, crossing, turning around.

She called Monday afternoon. "Would you like some company?"

She bought two raisin pecan scones and two coffees at Annabel's on Hudson Street and came up wearing blue jeans, T shirt, heavy leather jacket, eyeglasses with clear frames. On Saturday night I had knelt at her feet and, while massaging them, looked up at her. "I have a fetish," I said.

"Feet?" she said.

"Eyeglasses," I said.

She was wearing those glasses, and I wore the

baseball cap she had said suited me. She set our snack on my folding card table covered with a tablecloth decorated with ferns and red berries. My head moved across the table's corner toward Saturday night's kiss. She stood me up and pushed me back onto the bed.

Our first chance encounter happened early one weekday morning. An innocent sun peaked over the horizon, beaming golden rays onto the tops of the Twin Towers. She was walking toward them, south along Hudson Street, on her way to the apartment she had sublet to her ex boyfriend. One of her cats stayed with him and she'd go over to feed, play, with her. I was crossing Hudson Street, heading for the river. Our bodies were about to converge, seal like two true lines emanating from the ends of the world. I stopped, called her name, stood back to take in more of her in her surroundings, the corner pizza place. She looked at me, fixed a blank look and kept walking. My body tumbled south toward hers, arms outstretched, head reeling from side to side, up at the sky.

Then there was the Monday night on my way to Chinatown in the rain and I recognized her slender back and fresh short haircut in an Indian restaurant where she had taken her brother for his birthday. She saw me blowing kisses through the glass. She stood up abruptly. Her brother sat still as a statue. The restaurant door opened which she held ajar with one hand. She was wearing tight blue jeans and a black, long sleeve sweater. No matter how she felt about my intrusion, she arched her back so as to thrust forward her breasts. She pointed her left forefinger at my chest. "Take a walk," she scowled. "This is my family."

Another Monday night I wasn't home to catch her seven o'clock phone call but I knew her message would be waiting. A few hurried sentences, promise of tomorrow. I did not turn on the lights so that I could see the red message light flashing to the beat of my heart. Her gravelly voice was filled with alarm. "Do not call back. Repeat: do not call back tonight or tomorrow."

I paced throughout the night, dagger in my gaucho belt, black leather half gloves, black Stetson. Her husband had seen us kissing by the planter, I thought. He kept her tied up with baling wire all of Sunday and Monday. As Tuesday morning dawned, I bounded onto Hudson Street and walked briskly to her building. She leaves for her college at noon so there was plenty of time to reconnoiter. The entire north face of her building is exposed, looks onto a garage. A planter hangs in her second floor translucent bathroom window. Her kitchen window looks onto Hudson Street and beyond to a chain linked playground with slatted wooden benches all around that afford a clear view of her front door. But with the approach of noon, I positioned myself closer, against the street lamp across from the garage. Two mechanics partially blocked my view of her door.

She came out holding a yellow briefcase and a brown paper bag of garbage. She looked down at the pail, tentatively lifted the cover then began the short walk to the corner, adjusting her eyes to the glare of the noon day sun, the mechanics, street traffic. My still black figure loomed into view. She slowed, mouth open. I broke from the street lamp and rushed across the street. "What happened?"

"What do you mean?"

"Last night. Your phone call. You're in trouble."

"Oh, that. My husband is expecting an important phone call today."

Danger still lay ahead, and so I accompanied her to

the subway. Waited outside while she bought the daily paper and a pack of gum. Descended with her into the subway and bought a token. She wasn't wearing makeup; she put it on on the train, the ferry. At the turnstile, I said, "You are beautiful without make up."

"Where are you going?"

"With you. On the train. The ferry."

"Go home," she said with a painful smile. "Get some sleep."

Her office hours end at four thirty. She takes a bus to the ferry, ten minutes. The ferry embarks from the slip at a quarter to five, and barring rough water in which case she hears the clanking of the buoy bells, barring the passage up river or out to the ocean of supertankers or luxury liners, the ferry glances the pilings on the Manhattan side at five after five. The #1 train is waiting and roars to Christopher Street in five minutes. She picks up her mail at her ex boyfriend's. My place is between her two addresses, and at five thirty she opens my street door and buzzes once. I'm home. She has flat feet and springs off each step with her entire foot, as much from her heels as from her toes. She ascends on a platform originating in the center of the earth. She's the full orchestra beneath the stage that rises, instruments finding their pitch, at the onset of the stage show. Her enormous decorated hat precedes her. Happy, expectant eyes. Spectacular nose. Parted red lips. Giddy smile.

Johnny

I'll take the train in broad daylight, then walk to his house from the station. This way his neighbors and body- guards can see that I'm up to no evil purpose. I'll walk slowly, even stop now and then and gaze up at the rooftops for pigeons, making an easy target of myself. I'll don a smile, indicating that I'm unafraid and have come on pleasant matters, family matters. I'll go bearing gifts. In one hand I hold a panettone, that fancy Italian bread filled with tiny fruits and raisins, and already I can see Johnny and his lady huddled in their kitchen flooded by the early morning sunshine, anxiously slicing off a few pieces, then toasting them lightly and buttering them.   In my other hand I hold a naked mozzarella, pure white, still juicy and swollen from its recent baptism in water. Later on, while actually handing it over, I'll titter that my nickname in the family was "Mootzie," after mozzarella itself. I'll wear a bright, close fitting suit, all the pockets smooth so that it looks like I'm not packing heat and I've just come up from Miami or Nassau or over from Naples. Standing on the edge of his lawn is a mailbox inscribed with the family name, and in the time it takes to say Giuseppe Garibaldi my legs go rubber and my heart races from the fear.

But somehow I make it up the winding flagstones to his great white front door. I have a choice between the bell and the black iron knocker. I press the bell once, just to hear the chimes behind the door. I'm going to tell him about the church in my neighborhood in New York that uses a tape recording of a bell to sound the hours and play our holiday songs. Wouldn't it be a fascinating caper, I'll proffer, to climb up the bell tower in the dead of night, steal the tape, and free up the bell, and ring it, ring it until it creates a tremendous ruckus, wakes up the priests and the Italians on Carmine Street and everybody else.

Johnny opens the door himself, having absolutely nothing to fear. He looks splendid in a green banlon shirt and yellow cardigan sweater. My eyes fight not to look below his belt, but sense that his pants and shoes are black. I gaze up at his hairline. It is beautiful, tracing a delicate, clean line along the upper reaches of his wide, low forehead. I think of his barber, his personal barber. I think of Albert Anastasia's barber. Albert's mistake was that he didn't have a personal barber. Imagine lying in a barber's chair, your friendly barber hovering over you with as much care and knowledge about you as your mother, his warm, soft, moist hands working over your face, and then he applies the steaming towel and everything goes dark and warm and comfortable like the womb, and then, boom! out fly your brains. Wonder if the barber was in on it.

Johnny's face is blank, a clean slate prepared as much for a laugh as murder. Our first shared look is hard, wildly physical, at the level of the *coglioni*, this is how Italian men know they are men. Light from our hearts shines up to our eyes when we are with our mothers and our children, and sometimes, after giving them a hard time, our women. My face animates with the camouflage of chatter. "You look great, John," I tell him. "Youthful, handsome."

He looks beyond me at the trees and parked cars. Without a word, and with a gallant sweep of his arm, he ushers me into the vast parlor. Again I have a choice, a choice of chairs, and I sit on the endless sofa in case he wants to sit next to me, which I secretly desire, so long have I been away from my own. He sits in a wing chair, crosses his legs. "So you're the kid who can't find his way uptown," he says.

"I don't understand, Johnny..."

"Years back, didn't Ice get you a job at the Police Gazette and you got lost and told the editor, and after he gave you a test and you didn't write a word, you told him you were still upset about getting lost?"

Ice was a Broadway bookie, Genovese's family, with literary connections. The mystery writer, Andrew Swank, was a good friend.

"Do you know what the editor wanted me to write about?"

"Vaguely," Johnny says.

"Marilyn Monroe is on a yacht fucking the skipper. I'm a spy, see everything through the stateroom porthole. I couldn't do that, Johnny. She was Joe's girl."

Johnny nods.

I murmur, "Jesus."

"Tazza di caffè?" Johnny offers.

"English, Johnny, English. This is America."

He clenches his jaw. "Cup of coffee?"

"Thank you."

Divining the Don's desire, a middle aged man wearing a white jacket carries in an old copper eight cupper with an elegant spout. Johnny and I are silent, respectful, during the man's labor of resting the silver tray on the glass coffee table. After we drink like kings, I move to the edge of the sofa. "When I saw your eyes on the cover of *The New York Times Magazine*," I begin, "I knew they could see into everything, even into my subconscious, and they cleansed it of its penchant for debunking my own, for creating the beautiful lie. Rather than the stereotype, I opted for the beautiful lie. Now I want the truth, what went wrong, Johnny, what went wrong with me?

"Instead of becoming a doctor or a businessman, I became a lover. I, a Brooklyn boy, born the same year as you, at the outset of the war, from a good family, father a doctor, half Sicilian, half Neapolitan, the Sicilian predominant in that it was handed down by my mother. Every day for the past nine years I sat alone with my notebooks and gave love away to strangers. No Puccini, no family, no *paisani*, alone and silent. My desk looked out toward the Hudson River, and on the sill was a white scalloped bowl replenished each day with fresh water for the sparrows.

"The brick wall held the Sicilian wheel faced with a three legged angel with two snakes draped around her neck, and also one of our flags, the red, white and green. Red for the fire of our volcanoes. White for our snow capped mountains. Green for our wooded hills. The flag was given to us either by the great Italian from Corsica, Napoleon Bonaparte, or by Dante Alighieri, who in Canto XXX of the *Purgatorio* clothes his Beatrice in red, white and green. Dante sees her for the first time where we see all our women, in the Earthly Paradise, on the threshold of Paradise itself into which our women usher us. Beatrice sits aloft on a *carrocio*, or war chariot, covered with flowers cast by the angels. Flowers are still falling all around in showers-- yet, inspired by love, Dante's eyes behold Beatrice veiled in white, cloaked in green, her gown the color of living flame.

"After bestowing the daily gift, I was still alone in a ramshackle pre-war building a block away from Christopher Street when I love women, Johnny, love them as much as my distant children and dead mother. My wife was a thin

Florentine girl with a shrill voice. Ice was her uncle. How did Don Vito let in a Florentine? One of my last images will be of the beautiful Christina on her back, her legs up, and she reaches out to me and says, 'Come to me, baby, come to me.' Then I took up with a woman who didn't speak English, let alone Italian. An elegant lady from Brazil, and while I was with her, I came to believe that the most beautiful image in the world is flying into Rio de Janeiro at the level of the sunrise, seeing that strip of russet on the horizon. I was happy in the airport bathroom washing and shaving in front of Brazilians because I knew that in three more hours I'd be in Buenos Aires, and instead of dancing the tarantella, I'd be dancing the tango in the Club Gardel."

Sambucca

Around eleven o'clock, after Lefty goes home, I meet my friend Jacob in the Caffè Dante for an espresso and Sambucca. Jacob is Israeli, around Lefty's age, thirty, and in all his years growing up on a kibbutz, fighting the Arabs on the Syrian border, painting in his loft on the Bowery, he had never heard of the Italian liqueur Sambucca, how well anise and coffee mix together for that sweet, strong taste. But since his friendship with me, Jacob cannot dissociate coffee from Sambucca, and Sambucca from me.

Even when he takes his coffee alone, Jacob tells me, he thinks of me and has it with Sambucca, and many times I have considered buying him a bottle so that he could have it in his home, but I've stopped short, deciding he should take that step himself.

"Two espressos with Sambucca," Jacob takes pride in telling the waitress, a foreigner herself but well acquainted with the liqueurs of all nations. "Do you want cannoli?" Jacob asks me.

"No, thank you," I say.

"I want. So that's two espressos with Sambucca and one cannoli," he amends to the waitress. "Ah, Sambucca..." he sighs, sitting back.

Jacob's English is still a kind of shorthand, a staccato of key words, and it bothers him especially when he's among strangers at an opening. He speaks Hebrew at home with his wife, Daphna, but she has more of a command of the English language, having been raised in the cosmopolitan city of Haifa. She studied painting at the *Beaux Arts* in Prague, here she met Jacob and fell in love, abandoned her ambitions and then, according to Jacob, followed him to

New York and insisted on living with him, eventually cajoled him into marrying her. I keep telling Jacob that, as far as I'm concerned, I don't care how he speaks English. I can see his heart in his eyes, in his bleeding eyes, and feel his thrill with new discoveries like Sambucca and my girlfriend through my descriptions of her.

Before I met Lefty, I used to go to Jacob's place of an evening but now, on those evenings I do not see her, I go to sleep early so that my sleep, my dreams, can beckon the new day, one that holds promise of seeing her. A quick espresso with Sambucca replaced my former visits to Jacob's, and I found myself telling him about her as a way of having her with me in the café and in places I had been before we met.

Of late, I've attempted some discretion in the kinds of things I tell Jacob about her. As my love deepened, it became one with the silent, natural order of things, the turning of day into night, night into day. Words, I found, could not capture the gravity of my feelings. It's like trying to describe the wonders of the world with one breath. I tried all the same with Jacob, exercising my English so that he could get a feel for its power and beauty. But then, to my great horror, I discovered that in general Israelis don't like American Jews, and American Jews don't like Israelis. The enmity between them rivals that of Sicilians and Neapolitans. Lefty is an American Jew, and the first thing Jacob wanted to know was her name. I thought that, in announcing it, I was adding sweet music to the air. Jacob's regard for me did not extend to relaying his racist sentiments. He relayed them, instead, through his wife, whom, he knows, I like. "Daphna hates American Jews," Jacob told me.

Then he decided that, since he doesn't see me as

much, our friendship suffered. We had time only for my sex life, which told him everything, augured even my future well being.

My fondness for Jacob extends to telling him a little.

Afterwards, he says, wincing, as if my girlfriend's fluids got mixed in with his espresso and Sambucca, "You do *that*!"

"Oh, yes," I respond with reserve. "Every Monday, Wednesday, Friday afternoon and Saturday evening I make a big *mangione*."

"*Mang...*" he attempts to repeat.

"*Mangione*. From the Italian verb *mangiare*, to eat."

Jacob titters. He likes the word. "Say again," he says.

"*Mangione*. A big feast. Don't you like to do that?"

"No, I never do that," he says seriously.

"Her pubic hair is like silk," I go on, "a web of red

silk, and her PH is perfect. Sweet. Redolent of nectar."

"Does she do that to you?"

"Yes, and she's wonderful. Her lips, her tongue, her hand work together in marvelous unison."

"I fool around," Jacob confesses, which I knew.

"What do you do with the women you fool around with?" I asked.

"I only let them do that to me." Then he looks away. Tears come to his eyes. He says clearly enough, "I don't feel passion for my wife."

Button Man

"My girlfriend, Johnny, thinks I'm a torpedo, a shooter...

"Well, yes, she *is* a comedian of sorts. In literary circles she's what's known as a black humorist...

"No, no, she's not a funny black girl. She's a funny Jewish girl. Get this. We were in bed, you know, afterwards. I was totally spent, ricotta through and through and, for all I knew, she had had a good time, too. She was in my embrace and then, out of the blue, I hear, 'You're my button. You're my button man.'

"She knows I'm Italian from my musical name and sometimes she hears operatic arias, but she also hears Steven Sondheim and Argentine tangos. She brings over the wine, mainly French Bordeaux, and I don't complain. I've told her very little about my past. In fact, I told her that even if my mother were alive, I wouldn't be eager to introduce them.

"I wanted to tell her square in the face that she had read me all wrong but her face was turned away, my mouth was lost in her beautiful red hair. The more I tried to free up my mouth, the more she strained her naked body away. I managed, nevertheless, to say with some indignance that in my entire life I had never killed anybody, nor did I know certain personages who could have somebody hit. 'I've never even held a gun,' I mumbled.

"She scrambled up and sat on my belly. Threw back her head and laughed uproariously. 'You misheard me, asshole,' she quipped. 'You're *my* button man, I said.'

"I focused on the possessive pronoun *my*. I was 'hers'. Of all the men in the world, *I* was the one who belonged to her. Pleased at arriving at this understanding because up till then she had not told me she loved me, I said, looking up into her glazed eyes, 'You are finally announcing your love for me. You love me.'

"'I never said I loved you,' she said.

"'You don't love me?' I asked.

"'I never said that either. You know,' she said, 'for a smart guy you're sometimes slow on the uptake.'

"Now, Johnny, you and me know that sometimes we Italian men feign that we're slow on the uptake. Especially with family and our women we pretend we're idiots, clinical morons, all for the purpose of eliciting kindness, gentleness. But we're really always a step ahead, aren't we? Fast on all takes, up, down, sidewise, inside out. While my girlfriend and I exchanged dialogue, I was reasoning that if her tag 'button man' was not couched in amorous terms, it had to be couched in political ones. She thinks I'm her own private assassin, I concluded. I'm willing to murder out of love for her, she believes. For my dream of a future together, our home. Which led me to say, 'I love you, would gladly die for you, but murdering for you is a different story. I won't murder your husband, because for all I know I may be in the midst of a marital squabble. And I won't murder a former lover who's blackmailing you, threatening now to blow your cover. I'll tell you what I *will* do, though: I'll *talk* to your blackmailer, and if he or she isn't Italian, such talk, I assure you, usually does the trick'--

"What's that, Johnny?...

"No, no, she doesn't have money. The blackmailer's trade is silence for sex, sex for silence. She's a writer, Johnny. She's poor. She has a thousand dollars in the bank, she told me. She doesn't even know how much her husband makes...

"Of course I believe her! I believe every word she

says. I believe, for example, that since the day she married, five years ago, her husband hasn't touched her. They sleep in the same bed, and still I believe her husband doesn't touch her...

"He's straight, yes. I asked her point blank about that, and she nodded, then looked away. The sadness in her face, tears welling up, told me she was telling the truth...

"I agree. He probably has a little something on the side, too...

"It was over a game they were playing in bed. At some point her husband announced: 'I'm never going to make love to you again.' The guy's kept to his word. He's half Italian, you know.

"The problem isn't belief, Johnny. It's understanding. Understanding what she means.

"She listened to the twists and turns of my

understanding of her epithet *button man,* shaking her head, smiling slightly. 'Forget it!' she finally said, and then reached down with her strong, sinewy arms and dug her nails into my skin. Her nails, the same chestnut red as her hair and her lipstick, cut swaths from my shoulders down to my wrists. I was lost again, this time inside her, but through the mist of my half closed eyes I saw that her left arm was raised, her hand clenched in a fist, and then slowly, one at a time while she sighed, she raised her long, beautiful fingers: first her pinkie, then her ring finger, then her middle finger, then her forefinger. It was afterwards again, and I asked her, 'What were you doing raising your fingers?'

"'I was ticking off my orgasms,' she explained. 'I hit four times. You pressed my button four times. You're my *button man.*'

"Finally, I understood. I was the one man in the

world who brought her her greatest pleasure. I was happy and made us gnocchi with broccoli rappé. I carried her plate to her on a silver tray. She sat up cross legged like a kid home sick from school. I sat at the edge of the bed.

"'How do you feel about marriage?' she asked, eating.

"'Oh, I would marry you,' I answered immediately, believing she had proposed. Then, Johnny, I pictured myself going fishing, and while I was out on the bay in my rowboat with outboard, she was writing her stories in her own special studio made of glass so that when she looked away, musing, she was also among the sap and bark of our trees, and if it so moved her, she could feel beyond the trees to our home, see me trundling up the gravel path to our front door, carrying the daily catch in my red, stringy fishnet bag.

"'How do you feel about marriage?' she repeated.

"'Why do you ask?' I was wise enough to say.

"She must have coveted my question because she said with considerable strength, 'I want to know how deep your commitment to me is. And I'm going to tell you this: if you marry me, you'll have to make love to me every night. Every single night.'

"I thought, I make love to her every Monday, Wednesday and Friday afternoon, and Saturday night. I could succeed on Tuesday, Thursday and Sunday, too. At least I'd try. I knew for certain that every night I would touch her skin. Fall asleep with my hand on her back, or on the ridge between her buttocks and her back, or around her waist, our legs entwined."

Dreams on Bleecker Street

I prefer telling relative strangers about my girlfriend because they do not own a sense of my history. They have only her, exalted praise and stark images of a mysterious, fascinating woman. Then these strangers can go and incorporate her into their dreams.

She's incorporated into the dreams of a semi invalid street vendor, Bobby Fontana, who, except when it rains and is freezing cold and on his artificial limbs he wobbles and vaults across the street to Zito's bread store where he sits in the rear in semi darkness, sits outside beside his table of wares on Bleecker Street between Seventh and Sixth Avenues, on the south side of the street where the sun does not shine, and so in order to conjure up the true color of her hair, I point to the piece of sky directly above us, as if the sun were ablaze there. On Sundays Lefty goes antiquing with her husband, and I go for a solitary walk. One Sunday I see on Bobby's table packages of women's panties fringed with lace and men's briefs with sturdy supports around the crotch. One artificial limb stands beside Bobby, resting against the dark building. He greets me with the customary Italian baby talk, "How ya *do*in'!"

"After a dinner at my place with a bachelor cousin and I continue to sit in my yellow armchair, tired, satisfied, she hurries across the room and throws herself down at my feet, and after I say, 'Well, how was it?' she takes my right hand and places four fingers in her mouth and sucks them. Then she says, looking up at me, 'All I want is to be alone with you.'"

"I've had a few of those," Bobby says. He's a mess:

matted, black oily hair, face bloated and red from Vodka and beer, and screwed up all the time in an infantile pout.

"But have you ever had a woman who hovers above you with her jaw clenched and full lips pressed together like she's a girl again, attempting to get through something difficult for the first time, while her lower parts contain all the knowledge and experience of all women in all of history, and then later, much later, she rises straight up and smiles, closes her eyes and spreads her arms like she's riding. She raises her long fingers, one, two, three, as many as four, ticking off her orgasms. Then she whispers, 'I want to feel you dripping down my thigh,' and I return, 'No, no...' And when I go soft, she's young and insatiable, she tells me, 'Put your fingers inside me and see if the liquid feels different after an orgasm.' And I do, until my fingers cramp, and I report to her, 'It bubbles, effervesces.'"

Bobby says, "I have this friend who works at the Pink Pussy Cat. She tells me that sales on vibrators have skyrocketed since AIDS and every other fucking thing..."

"A vibrator rests in an unopened box amid her books, manuscripts and cats--a constant reminder how easy it would be to finish herself off, and conduct, in fact, the entire technical enterprise. But she doesn't want it easy. She wants it hard and real. She wants human fire."

"Do me a favor," Bobby pouts. "I heard there's a vibrator on sale for thirty dollars and you can give massages with it, too. Go to the Pink Pussy Cat and check it out for me."

The Widows

"I want to go home, Johnny. That is, I want to make a home with a woman I love. My home doesn't have to be in Brooklyn or Queens or on Staten Island. It could be anywhere on the face of the earth, and I'll buy nice things and learn to care for them. Cook and in my garden grow broccoli-rappe' and arugula. Despite my age, I'm even thinking of having children. Tell me what to do."

Johnny uncrosses his legs and straightens up enough for his right hand to sail into his pants pocket. He withdraws a wad of cash.

"No, Johnny, please. Not between us. Money must not pass between us."

He pauses, conceding I may be right, but then simultaneously his eyes open wide and his sharply defined lips begin to mouth a word. For emphasis, I suspect, for highlighting the word's importance. From its first harsh consonant, I know what the word is and immediately I feel all its lethal implications. I blanch, cringe low on the sofa. My heart pounds in terrifying anticipation. Johnny's lips together with his taut mouth take on the shape of a long bow which shoots the word directly into my heart: "J...o...b".

While my heart bleeds, a handyman carries in a telephone, one of those outsize antique telephones, ornate and bright. He holds out the receiver for Johnny. The desired party is already on the line.

Though Johnny is only nine feet away and I can see he's talking, his lips are moving, I cannot make out a word. His lips stop. He holds up the receiver like a torch. His eyes slowly turn on me, and he says peremptorily, "Maître d' at

44

the Club Elegante. Ocean Parkway, Brooklyn. You start tomorrow night, six o'clock."

I die, and then, suddenly, everything grows calm and I see it all. A slight smile comes over my pale visage, and with eyes aglow from the celestial light I thank Johnny from the bottom of my wounded heart. "But it won't work," I go on to tell him. "Oh, I'd wear a fine tuxedo and every night a fresh carnation. Come eight o'clock my face would beam, as it beams now, and I'd stand tall and straight and glide amid the tables and chairs. But do you know what would happen? I'd pick out the widows. I'd pick them out and devote all my attention to them. They'd arrive in groups, at least in pairs, accompanied by their brothers and their brothers' wives, by old married friends of their deceased husbands. I'd know the young widows by their dates, small time hoods, burly, adorned with gold, thin mustaches, short. The widows, their hair would be done up in silver, and they'd wear sack like dresses glittering with sequins to deflect the eye from the thick set of their bodies. Atop their heads I'd see the nimbus of love left behind by grief. No amount of makeup and fragrance and show of fun would hide the pain in their faces, their cried out eyes. I'd see the trace of tears. The purple color around their eyes. *I'd* cry. I'd place my arm around their shoulders and, while ushering them to tables surrounding the dance floor, I'd manage to say softly that they could talk to me of their grief. Throughout the night, I'd pull up a loose chair and sit beside them. We'd talk of other things: children, volunteer work, getting in shape, the value of sweet memories, the prospect of new love. Whenever the band struck up a foxtrot, I'd approach smiling, arm extended. Silent, in a light embrace, the widows and I would dance the evenings away."

The Sabbath

"**A** Jewess," she calls herself with venom and heart, even though she doesn't go to temple or back home for the high holy days. She's spent the last fifteen Christmas Eves with an old Irish Catholic boyfriend and his buddy, an Italian who lives and cooks on Sullivan Street. On Christmas Eve, I pass my mother's first home across from St. Anthony's church, and then I pass my grandfather's tenement on Mulberry Street. I revealed my ritual to her in the hope she would invite me along to the Italian's.

"I prefer one on one," she said.

She's discovering the ways she's a Jewess with her novel and, when it's finished, she's taking Yiddish lessons at the Workman's Circle, where I go for my teeth. She's discovering the ways she's a Jewess one on one with my goy

Italian cock, hungering after the probe that will light the way of her quest, burn out, explode her ignorance by stopping up her mouth, filling her gut and her hand.

Seeking to protect me from American Jews, my friend Jacob mumbled, "Bridge. You are a bridge for her," meaning that for my Jewess I am a suspension over the river, a suspended crossing erected by us only for her. The bridge claws, arches, spans the mass of her past and her future. She saunters across with her heavy Mae West step, eyes crossing down at the ships coming and going, kicking up her polka dot pocketbook with her muscular thigh. Waiting on the other side, smiling, is her realized self, an address, commercial publisher, foster children, renewed husband.

Jacob's mistress is the aerobics instructor at our gym. Though they are young and in Olympic shape, their passion flagged after a week. Jacob sought to buoy it by thinking of me, of her. "I don't understand," he sighed with universal despair. "It's not like you and Lefty."

His mistress is an Italian Olympian from Brooklyn, lives alone, has all the easy time a man could ask for, but I said only, "I don't know, Jacob. It's said that Jewish girls got permission from their mothers. But I really don't know. God only knows."

Yahweh rested from creating Heaven and Earth in all their array on the seventh day. Her husband's seventh day, his Sabbath, is Sunday. He likes to brunch, read the papers she bought on Saturday night. She lolls around in bed, naked. "He wouldn't dare," she responded to my questioning look, her eyes fixed God knows where. After brunch, if the sun is shining, they stroll along Hudson Street, and sometimes he places his arm around her shoulders. "And I respond," she told me. She rests her head, her pyre of hair illuminated its true color by the sun, in the crook of his arm, and they go on their way.

She takes it easy on Saturday, I noted. Writes letters, Xeroxes, does the laundry. I wanted to have some fixed time together, so I suggested, "Let's spend every Saturday evening together."

She agreed. "I'll call you first."

"You can call if you wish," I said, "but you really don't have to. I'll be here every Saturday night at six o'clock. I'll be here every Saturday night unless I'm dead. If I'm dead, I'll still be here. If I do not respond immediately to your buzz, come in with the keys I gave you. I'll be in our bed facing the wall, turn me over and you'll see a smile. My last words were, 'Please tell me you love me,' and you remained true to yourself and I smiled and died."

So as not to miss her call on Saturday, so as to be

able to say nonchalantly, "I have everything," every Saturday morning at daybreak while the farmers with fresh faces truck down their produce, I take up my red fishnet shopping bag and scurry to the open air market at Union Square, where I smell, touch, buy our lettuce, scallions, radishes, mushrooms. "You are my dessert," she told me, and so south and east to Vaneiro's for the next best thing, *sfogliatelle* and *cannoli* made overnight. On the way home, Tutta Pasta for the spaghetti and Parmesan cheese. Zito's for the Italian bread. Faicco's for the mozzarella, anchovies, black olives. The Candle Shop. Hurtle the four flights not to an empty place but to her voice screaming for me. I pick up the phone.

"It's me," she says. "What should I bring?"

"I have everything."

Once she said, "I begin to get excited at three o'clock." At three o'clock, I break open the card table, our dinner table, set it with my mother's linen, initialed napkins. Tolle silver, Noritake china rounded with red and white roses. At precisely six o'clock, her left hand grasps the doorknob of the street door. A hard door but her arms are strong, thin but strong, she curls fifty pound barbells. By the time this old, brown door closes slowly on its tight hinge, she's taken two quick steps into the box-like, stifling hallway. Now she does something odd. When she reaches her destination, a person, a place, she does a stutter step, as if her destination were somewhere beyond. She stutter steps before the panel of buttons at her right. She raises her left arm. Her left, red forefinger breaks from the others and points and moves through the stale air to the lower left bell at the level of her waist. She rings once, a buzz, low and raspy, like her voice. As she climbs, a gray veil envelops us, pulls us toward each other, her arms reaching up four flights, my arms reaching down. A soprano begins singing "Ave

Maria." Lefty's hair catches fire. The first sun sits atop the

horizon and casts a rosy hue on Paradise. Fish jump out of

the water and take legs. The atoms of the cold ancient rock

and of the layer of earth just beneath the barren plain

coalesce, tighten, warm.

From the Shadows

Johnny closes his eyes in disgust, turns his head away at a downward angle. He twists with impatience in his chair. He says, completely annoyed, "Now I have to call the guy back and tell him you're not taking the job. You know, you're one big fucking pain in the ass!"

I lower my head in despair, close my eyes and glimpse the infinite darkness. The same infinite darkness we all see, Johnny sees. When I open my eyes, I see in front of me an infinity of spaghetti bleeding with marinara sauce, surmounted by a congregate of meat balls and sausages. I sense a presence hovering over me. The man in the white jacket who brought in the coffee on a silver tray. He says, holding up a heaping tablespoon, "*Formaggio?*"

"Pardon me?"

"Cheese? Some Parmesan cheese?"

"Oh, I love Parmesan cheese. But, you see, I can't eat the spaghetti."

"I never heard of such a thing," the man says. "An Italian who can't eat pasta. My wife made fresh."

"I'm allergic to wheat," I explain. "The allergy came upon me quite inexplicably at the age of forty. Please thank your wife for me."

"Jesus," Johnny murmurs.

I nod, and then I tell him that I've been this way from the very beginning. For the first three years of my life I cried day and night, sometimes eighteen hours at a stretch. My Uncle Freddie gave me Phenobarbital. I cried twenty hours. I cried so hard that a coin had to be fastened to my belly button to keep my stomach from bursting. My ears looked a little large, maybe they were weighing down my head. My ears were tied back with a string. My mother took me on a train to a famous pediatrician in New York. He examined me from my toenails to the hair follicles on top of my head. "He's a textbook specimen," this doctor defined me.

"But he cries twenty hours a day! And for no reason at all. He eats and shits like a horse." My mother was searching for some emotional disturbance. But we're talking 1943. The war was in full swing, who cared about psychiatry?

"Well, let's see…he's not circumcised. Have you been cleaning it?"

"Cleaning it!" echoed my mother, insulted. "Four times a day I roll back the skin and oil that little dingle of his with cotton."

"He's just a cry baby. One day he'll stop," the doctor

concluded.

I stopped crying while my mother rocked me in her soft, thick arms. She stopped to let down and put up her hair. Sensing that I was let go, I bolted, stiffened and kicked my legs. Flailed my arms at the thin air and twisted my wrists and screamed.

One night around three a.m., I stopped crying and dribbled the word, Stick. "Stick, stick..." I repeated. My parents remembered that that afternoon I had played with a stick in my grandmother's backyard, her rose garden. It was overrun with vines sprouting prominent sharp thorns. The stems of the long pink and red roses also sprouted thorns. The place was dangerous but you knew what was what. If you touched a thorn, it hurt and you bled. Only a little fellow could ensconce himself back there. Vines and flowers overhung the narrow, whitewashed walkway. There I sat, peaceful, surrounded by the beauty and sweet fragrance of roses, playing with my stick.

My father put on his beige raincoat over his silk pajamas and went out into the darkness. Crossed the avenue, the shadows beneath the el. The door to my grandmother's house was open. Bensonhurst wasn't called *God's Country* for nothing. Ducking low, my father scoured the yard for a stick. He found it lying in a ray of moonlight.

I stopped crying for longer periods outside than in, and so my mother walked me in my carriage outside in the sun. If she wheeled me in the direction of the trains, I stopped crying even when my carriage was still. A train passed every ten minutes or so, 24 hours a day. My mother turned the carriage around and tilted it so I could see the trains in the full glory of their roar and speed. I googooed and drooled, tried to get up. A serious look came over my face as my deep set hazel eyes followed each window, each passing car. If the traffic on New Utrecht Avenue was slight, say after a heavy snowfall, my mother burrowed the carriage through the snow and stopped in the middle of the street to show me the trains from directly underneath, from the shadows, up through the wooden slats. When a train passed, sparks rained down, diffusing before they reached us. For a few seconds up there, it was a shower of stardust.

The Paramour

12:30. Monday, Wednesday, Friday afternoon. She's married. She'll be here in a half hour.

I get up. The desk chair topples over. Pace to the yellow armchair, which doesn't move of its own accord. I have to have something to talk about in the first stages of our embrace.

"Pedestrian," she calls such attempts.

"Grounding," I call them. She doesn't want me to fly out through the skylight. She wants me down here, in my single bed, inside her hard and hot.

12:33. Pace back to the desk. I'll tell her about the good time I had, "fun," out on the street with Bobby Fontana. Relay my conversation, "stimulating," with my friend Jacob. All this so that I can conclude, "You were the central character, the sun, filling the street and the café with your light, just as you fill me now."

"There you go going romantic on me."

"Romantic" is beginning to sound like an evil word.

12:35. Progress into the kitchen, where everything looks and feels foreign, as if in my entire life I've never seen a glass or a fork. My trembling hand reaches for the medicine bottle concealed in a demitasse cup standing idly among the groceries. The bottle is narrow, rather short, only because the elixir it contains is in the form of tiny yellow pills. The bottle cap is a lively green, the color of hope, and rises above the coffee cup so I can see it, touch it, try to align the grooves to open it. This I must do in order to pick out a pill and take it, which in turn will give me the hardness to satisfy her.

After I revealed my symptoms to the doctor, I was

prepared to drop my pants so that he could examine my muscle, determine whether it had the capability any longer of filling with bone. I was prepared to stimulate myself behind a curtain. Or maybe the doctor, a blond haired, virile looking young man, had some artificial means to stimulate me, a viscous suction apparatus, and then once I was hard, quickly, he would x ray the bone for fractures. Even a hairline fracture would explain why as soon as it hits her pubic hair, it goes soft. The body's defense mechanism knows that sustaining hardness could compound the fracture, deepen it.

But the doctor did not ask me to drop my pants, nor did he probe my genitals beneath my pants, beneath my purple briefs, with his gloved hand. Instead, he took my blood pressure, then pronounced it was that of a young buck. He listened to my heart and said the beat was rather rapid, nearly a hundred. A wonderful blood pressure together with a rapid heartbeat could indicate some stress, he chanced. Finally, he listened to my stomach, listened a long time, and I was surprised because I had not complained of indigestion. "It's soft," he said of my stomach, which I took to mean healthy, "but I hear tremors," he added with concern. "Definitely stress."

What was happening was that my desire, originating in my stomach, was being effaced by these tremors like mountain rock washed away inch by inch by the lapping of sea water over a period of centuries, so that by the time my desire descended to my muscle, it was weak, depleted, a yelping child with the memory of a man, and simply did not have the strength to initiate the growth of bone.

"One half hour before your girlfriend comes over," the doctor instructed, "take one of these." He made out the prescription in triplicate to convince the druggist that the panacea was indeed the work of a physician, not a god.

"These" is a controlled substance called "Xanax."

12:42. Twenty Xanaxes spill out into my sweaty palm. I pick one out, pop it into my mouth. No need for water. Peristalsis will wash it down.

Xanax, the Sicilian champion come to fight for the Greeks, steps out from the ranks, and with a booming voice heard all around the countryside calls out the Trojan champion.

"Stressimpotence! Stressimpotence! Let's you and me settle this dispute with hand to hand combat. Winner take all!"

Moments later, the great city gate opens, but it does not dwarf the mighty Trojan, who emerges in full battle armor, wielding an ax, slinging his net. Behind

Stressimpotence, radiant in his massive shadow, is his Queen, naked, arms open, smiling. Xanax wears only a loincloth, his sweating muscles gleam, and in his shadow cowers his frightened little King. Xanax goes unarmed except for his hands and eyes, which in the face of battle turn black and shoot flames. At the sight of them, Stressimpotence drops his arms and flees. Xanax, proud, turns and leaves the field, winning the day.

12:46. Touch myself. Hard, the muscle contiguous with the desire in my stomach.

12:46:52. Touch myself. Soft. My apartment door opens into the kitchen. It is here where we embrace. She has her leather jacket on. Leather and her skin are one. She surrenders her body.

"I was never with a woman who surrendered her body so completely."

"Oh?"

"I was never with a woman who surrendered her body so completely."

"What is it about the kitchen you like so much?"

"Wherever you are is the right place for me. Other than that, I don't know."

"Freud."

"Freud?"

"Your mother."

But that isn't my mother cooking in an open satin robe. I come up behind her, kiss her neck. Right hand on her left breast, left hand on her right breast. She cranes her neck, lips parted.

"Can I make love to you like this?"

"You don't have to ask. I want to be the best piece of ass you ever had."

In our embrace, I whisper, "You are. You are the best piece of ass I ever had."

12:51. Into the bathroom. Her satin robe rests on a hanger caressed by a hook. I kiss the robe. Stare at and pity the clasps that will never join their mates.

"I'm beginning a new cycle with you. This morning I awoke with the name of our first child, 'Jules'."

"Buy a plant and call it 'Jules'."

"Yesterday I had a lot of fun in the street with Bobby Fontana, the street vendor."

"I've seen him walk without his artificial limbs."

"Me, too. I've seen him walk without his artificial limbs, too."

"He was a boxer, you know. Lost the use of his legs that way."

12:57. My hand hovers over the buzzer.

"I'm so surprised over the trouble between Israelis and American Jews."

"Do you want to know why? American Jews feel that Israelis are too belligerent in their political positions, and Israelis feel that American Jews are cowards, wimps. If they were real Jews, they'd go to Israel. Tell your friend Jacob to go back to Israel."

"In the café he told me he likes women only to do *that* to him. I don't think he likes women."

"He doesn't like women."

1:00. Her ring. My buzz. She's in. Open the kitchen door.

A dying person tries to find a comfortable position in which to die. My father sat at the edge of his bed, his head down between his knees. I try to find a comfortable position from which to view the appearance of her red hair.

Stand in front of the yellow armchair. Listen, watch.

Up two flights, three. Her steps are steady, rhythmic. She's a petite woman, my girlfriend. Five feet, two inches, about a hundred pounds, and not an inch of fat anywhere.

Her arms and legs are thin, strong. Her hands are large, her fingers veiny and long.

Her footsteps are those of a giant.

Song of the Castrato

I'm reluctant to tell Johnny any more about my girlfriend because as soon as I open my mouth about her, I lose all control. My neck rolls as do my eyes. I hyperventilate. My lungs cannot keep pace with the feelings in my heart. My voice changes. Lefty says that I talk the way Frank Sinatra sings, but she doesn't hear me talk about her, doesn't hear my mellifluous baritone transform to a castrato, an impassioned castrato who, after he sings his aria of unrequited love, is so overwrought that all that remains to him are tears in his eyes, pain in his heart, utter exhaustion. He cannot remember the words. They are not meant for now. They are meant for a millennium from now and a different place, one where there are no mountains to echo, just a vast, desolate plain, and every year or so, about fifty feet in the air all across the plain, the words play calm and clear, soothing reminder of one man's ancient love for a woman.

But maybe Johnny will understand. He has loved. He loves his wife so much he'd kill for her. And so, after hearing me, he'll seek to contain my exultation in the here and now. He'll smile slightly, rise from his chair and come over to me, tap my cheek and say, "After all you've said about your girlfriend, she sounds wonderful and I'd like to meet her."

"Oh, definitely, I'd have to say," and then the next Monday, Wednesday or Friday afternoon I'd tell her first thing, excited, "Johnny wants to meet you."

"No problem," she's likely to respond, or "Don't make appointments for me."

In the latter case, what do I do? Cancel the

appointment? Coax her into going, stating unequivocally that among Italians one must always consummate the promise, that my very life may hinge upon it because with a man like Johnny, you never know what trips his trigger?

She will remain true to her feelings and mood, one reason I love her more than my life. She knows this and will acquiesce and, if it turns out that she doesn't take to him, she will not say, "I don't like you, you're a bum!" She will, instead, say very little. Nothing, in fact. She will sit demurely in her thigh length, leopard skin skirt and halter cut at the midriff, black stockinged legs crossed, an attentive, intelligent, unreadable look on her face, which for an Italian male is worse than a show of hostility.

Johnny will grow nervous and look to me for an explanation. It's not polite to bring the unfriendly into the parlor. I'll raise my brows, shrug my shoulders, and right there make apologies in the past tense, as if she had died and we were doing the autopsy.

"A new book was coming out and she was under a lot of pressure. Reviews, book parties, readings."

"She was just about to get her period, and one of her PMS'S was suicide."

"What could a Jewish girl from Long Island know about Italians from Brooklyn? She married a half Irish, half Italian from Jersey, who on his wedding day bought a newspaper and a pack of gum, went home and read and chewed, then went to sleep."

Lesson on Paradise Island

"Listen, Johnny, there's this Italian kid professor who's been mouthing off about his former life as a thief at literary functions and in the same breath puts down his wife like she's some bimbo or something. *Para brutto*, Johnny. It looks bad for you, me, all of us. Why, why do we put down our women in public? Do we feel we are not good enough for them?"

"The kid's name? Ted Nardack. Sounds more Polish than Italian, I know, but it was one of those mix-ups at Ellis Island where the indignant American clerk with the bloated dough face, tiny cap and clear spectacles hears Teodoro Nardacci and writes Ted Nardack. Don't kid yourself that this kind of thing was an aural misconnection. Americans don't want to know about our vowels. Even the great

DiMaggio, Sicilian as you and me, they call 'the Yankee Clipper,' while hot dog and apple pie Babe Ruth they call 'the Bambino.' By all rights it should be the other way around."

"What's that, John? DiMaggio played for the Yankees? Well, so did Babe Ruth. Anyway, about this big-mouth kid...

"If he kept his mouth shut, nobody would even know he's Italian. His work itself would be enough to elevate and dignify us. He got a boat load of cash from Giovanni Agnelli, the Fiat tycoon..."

"Fiat? Fiat is one of those toy Italian cars they need to squeeze through the narrow, winding, cobblestone streets, hold the tortuous turns on the open passes spiraling up the mountains to the villages. Your limo can't fit on the streets of Corleone, would fly off the cliffs.

"With the imported money, the kid puts together an

anthology of Italian writing: short stories, essays, novel excerpts, things like this. Next year he's doing autobiographies. He calls and says, 'Do you have an autobiography?' Word gets around the colleges and he's invited to read and preside over panel discussions. But the problem is, Johnny, he has this fascination with his father's line of work that could upset irrevocably the important work he's doing. The old man was a loan shark, independent, too independent, and was whacked in his apartment building, in the lobby. Expired in his son's arms. The kid, naturally, doesn't forget, but as he grows he's unable to separate his love for his father and his sorrow and the image of his father letting blood in his arms, from his father's line of work and his enemies. Everything gets mixed up, confused, which doesn't make for a genuine effort either in the life of a true criminal or in the life of a true cultural pioneer.

"So what does the kid do? He starts hanging around bars on the South Side, seeking out the types. Steals a few armfuls of silk suits from off the rolling racks. One arrest but makes a connection who squashes the sheet. While he's going a little crazy, thanks to his blessed mother, the kid studies, studies hard. Forges an avenue or two through his thick skull. Puzo's 'The Godfather' comes out, and the kid studies that. Again he calls me: 'That book and its ramifications were the turning point of my life.'

"Exactly what these ramifications were escape me now, but one of them had something to do with the sudden realization that he could use the crime in his father's blood, his blood, and the blood in his culture as grist for the academic mill, and in his writing, too, as a tension, conflict. At the same time, in his real life, he begins to sort out images from their false, dangerous projections. Feels his heart, that it's capable of remorse, forgiveness, universal brotherhood. He graduates college with flying colors and goes for his Masters Degree. Does a paper on Hemingway. His sponsor, an American, berates him for being too emotional. The kid calls, fills my ears, and I tell him: 'Your sponsor is absolutely right. Hot on hot's no good, kid. When your subject is hot, you have to be cool.' Stuff like this I tell him.

"He takes my advice and gets the paper through. Acquires his Master's and a teaching job. He's eternally indebted to me, he tells me, so maybe he'll listen some more. Sometimes I think it'll be easier to get him a full professorship than have him clam up. Listen to this.

"He's invited to a college near me, across the river in Jersey. Hoboken, I think. First class event: elevated stage, standing mikes, glasses of water and a videotape machine worked by an emaciated, awkward black fellow attached to the college somehow who at first appeared marginal, you know, a little crazy, but who turned out to be truly interested and bright. Packed auditorium, including a Spanish professor from Montclair State and a black professor from Rutgers. Throughout the reading, at which I read, too, you could hear a pin drop, then the audience asked lots of intelligent questions during the panel discussion on the origins of modern Italy, which the kid led. But then about a dozen of us of all nationalities and color go to this cozy Italian restaurant. What does the kid do straightaway? Before the antipasto arrives, he conjures up the scene where he connected with the fence who took the silk suits. Then in the same breath he invokes an ugly picture of his wife who's back home caring for their kids. One of those midwestern types, dairy fed, strong backed, blonde. The kid's actual words were 'a blonde with big tits.'

"The whole table looked at me with startled, satisfied eyes, as if to say, 'You see, sooner or later the true Italian color comes out.'"

"Why did they look at me? I had adopted the appropriate public posture, silent as a snake, and the dignified silence spoke of pride and admiration for the kid. And I was hungry like everybody else, digging into the prosciutto and olives.

"So what do you say, Johnny? Let's take this kid aside and talk to him, put the arm on him a little bit. Let's you and me and a couple of the boys take him away for a weekend from the environs of his dark memories and his misrepresented wife. We'll fly down to Paradise Island, and over cocktails on our veranda overlooking the palm trees and emerald ocean, you place your arm gently around the kid's shoulders, muss up his hair a little like he's a boy again, and softly, your compassionate eyes staring into his frightened ones, you say, 'We understand about your father, that the image of his bullet riddled body is all powerful, that you feel profound pity and filial love and well founded hatred and bitterness and shame. But all this can dwell inside side by side. Keep them the fuck that way. And your wife, it looks funny how you're talking about her. She's loyal and hard working, supportive and, from all reports, beautiful. You secretly love her, don't you? See... It's alright to proclaim your love for her to the world. Finally, remember, always remember, that you're a professor now and not a thief. For the time being, we have to tolerate our crime and our culture, but your job is to promote culture, not the crime.' Here, Johnny, I suggest you make a wide sweep of your free arm, taking in all of us and the trees and the ocean, and your face suddenly goes dead, and you say in your most ominous, sweet tone: 'Do this for me. Do this for Johnny,

at least until the likes of us are gone. OK...? Good. Now

let's all go to the jai alai games.'"

As You Do

At the height of every summer, beautiful women from around the world traveled here with their hopes and dreams packed in their manuscripts. From Wales and South Africa they came, Russia, Canada and Westchester, leaving behind husbands, lovers, children. And once in the literary mecca, who did these women look to to fulfill their dreams? The likes of Ralph Stiller, the likes of me.

"So I had power, too, Johnny. I had a lifetime invitation to teach at this prestigious writers conference here in town."

Professor Emeritus Ralph Stiller founded the conference over thirty years ago. From thirty years ago until the end of his life, Ralph had his pick of these beautiful, adoring women. He married four of them, but each marriage lasted only a few years, about the time it takes for a young, starry eyed woman to realize that her idol is simply a man, and that's that.

"When I lecture, John, I pace. Back and forth, head down, oblivious to everything, to skirts hiked in the front row, legs crossed. Then one sunny afternoon, step, a pair of eyes blazing into me..."

Scorching July day after day, I felt the eyes penetrating me, following me, a powerful magnetic beam drawing me to the source. Now I paced, mumbled and also gazed along the rows ascending gradually toward the back windows and up to the ceiling. Finally, scanning the very top row, I found them, the eyes. Startled, unblinking, horrified eyes set against a sheet of brilliant sunlight between grand wavy curls and thick, puckered lips caked with icy lipstick.

Students had their pick of professors for private conferences. The Eyes picked me. After receiving an offer to move into a Beverly Hills mansion, I began holding my conferences in relative public. Pat Boyle's husky voice took over from her eyes. She suggested that we confer in a cafeteria style restaurant a short way from the university proper. Still a public place, a pleasant tourist kind of walk, and there was something particular about me that had to do with her story, a tragic story, I divined, one that was ablaze in her heart.

Most writing students put too much in the first paragraph. They also say too much in the first minute.

"I hate my job as a computer programmer. My novel is the search for the mother I never knew. I love dogs. My husband plays golf all the time. The novel begins with a trip to the cemetery. My father's friends out in Sag Harbor are friendly."

"Beginning at your mother's gravesite sounds like a good idea," I tried.

Her eyes opened wide again. Any words of mine uttered anywhere prompted a transition, a startling transition that only her eyes could make. Now in the cafeteria, facing me, she found their mirror, the words, which she strung slowly along the tensile line of her stare:

"I...want...to...do...as...you...do."

"And what is that?" I had to ask, mesmerized, forgetting momentarily all of my history.

"Publish...edit...teach in a university."

Ralph Stiller's fourth wife was also his conference assistant, and over the winter the marriage ended. Over lunch Ralph said, "I'm interviewing women."

"A conference assistant shouldn't be hard to find," I

ventured.

"An assistant is not what I'm interviewing for. I'm interviewing for a wife."

That's exactly what I heard, "interviewing for a wife." Then, in a seamless transition, Ralph listed the candidates thus far: a short story writer/teacher and an art history student. "I've already hired a new conference assistant," he added by way of addressing my misdirection. "Pat Boyle."

Over the winter she revealed to Ralph what she had revealed to me, that her husband plays golf all the time, the marriage was breaking up, and at the same time she was searching for her mother and had ambitions. Ralph pounced on the whole package, especially the ambitions, needing strong willed women who didn't distinguish between talent and ambition so he wouldn't have to trump up the talent part in the event she didn't have any.

At the next conference, the next summer, Pat Boyle and I had occasion to talk. Administrative details such as time and place of lectures, private conferences, my home address and telephone number.

My doorbell rang. I buzzed, thinking it's the mailman, but my mailman wore sneakers, not high heels. From the top landing, I saw Pat Boyle climbing up, holding a thick manila envelope. I greeted her cordially and invited her to sit in my yellow club chair. With the advent of summer I had taken out my vinyl beach chair, which I unfolded and sat in across the room. Pat Boyle's legs were at the level of my eyes. Crossed, meaty legs. She strung together two sentences that made sense. "I'd like you to critique my novel. How much will you charge?"

"How many pages?"

"Five hundred and…"

"Four thousand dollars," I said softly, then shifted my beach chair toward the view out the window, the flourishing wild tree that over the years had grown up from the courtyard, the sparrows playing, splashing in the bowl of water on the sill. Suddenly, I felt a pair of strong hands on my neck, my back.

Ralph Stiller got wind of the rest of the afternoon. I'm fired, out of the conference. Pat Boyle's in.

In his youth, Ralph Stiller had cut such a handsome figure that e.e. cummings propositioned him. e.e. was giving a reading, spotted Ralph in the audience, and then over the wine and cheese whispered to him, "You are my next lover."

Ralph had to explain that he was not that way. In all the years that followed, he was still not that way. Even his view of the statue of Garibaldi in Washington Square Park was heterosexual.

While Ralph and I were still friends, he used to invite me to Arturo's on Sullivan Street. Ralph had his own special table in the back room which, he informed his guests, was once a bowling alley and also the room where Eugene O'Neil ate. My route to the restaurant took me past Garibaldi's statue, and one lunch I mentioned as much. Ralph responded, "Do you know what my students say?"

"What do your students say?"

"That when a virgin passes the statue, Garibaldi's saber rattles."

I didn't tell Ralph that Garibaldi was a guerrilla chieftain always on the run, spent his adult life among veterans of guerrilla wars from around the world, and never as much as met a virgin. The Garibaldi anecdote was not about statues, it was about Ralph's transition to his new wife.

All interviews had been conducted, he said, and he had made his choice: the art history student. A fair, freckled twenty year old. "And Joan is a virgin," Ralph added, smiling.

In his mid seventies when I last saw him, and like Hemingway had fought in the Spanish Civil War, Ralph Stiller still cut a handsome figure. Tall, lean, mustache, stentorian voice shimmering with passion. Like Hemingway again, Ralph was a fisherman. He fished in the trout streams of Vermont, where he kept a cabin. Unlike Hemingway, Ralph didn't write fiction, he taught it and, by the way, didn't feel like a desperado accepting good money and inexpensive, elegant housing and full health benefits for teaching something he didn't know how to practice. *I* felt all these things. But when he retired, Ralph said, he was going to devote the rest of his days to writing. He planned to retire after the conference at which Pat Boyle was still a student.

But then, as often happens, he fell in love instead. "I'm breaking Joan in sexually," he said, still smiling.

"Wonderful," I said.

Before Joan, Ralph went on to say, he had to be stimulated anally with an electric rod. That's exactly what I heard: "stimulated anally with an electric rod." Joan aroused him naturally with the ardor of her passion. And she loved him. She wanted to have children with him. "I feel bad I have so little of a future to offer her," Ralph said.

"Future!" I bellowed. "Joan can die before you. And who eats better than you, you old geyser."

At our last dinner, Ralph complained that he wasn't writing. "Joan won't let me out of bed until three in the afternoon." As if she manacled his free arm to the bedpost, like Balzac's wife, until Honoré finished his daily quota of ten thousand words. Then Ralph said, "Can Joan and I stay at your place next weekend? It's so romantic there, like a villa overlooking the Mediterranean, quiet except for the sparrows chirruping, trees rich with foliage, the brick wall, fireplace..."

"Sure, Ralph," I said, "you and Joan can stay at my place. The bed doesn't have a post, though," I added, smiling, and wasn't smiling when I said, "Put aside the idea of writing. Returning the love of a woman like Joan is a far, far better way to end one's days. Yes," I said as we parted, "love and work at conceiving a child together."

The Reason of Tears

Johnny uncrosses his legs, then crosses them anew. His forearms rest on the wings of his chair. His hands hang down, fingers spreading, reaching. "So why do you think you cried so much?"

"Just a cry baby, like the doctor said. Now doctors would say I was colic."

"Colic schmalic! Doctors circumcised us, what was that, hygiene! Next you'll tell me in your first five years you cried enough for a lifetime."

"Haven't shed a tear since."

Johnny kicks the floor with his left heel. The momentum carries his foot up into the glass coffee table, knocking off the top of the crystal candy dish filled with wrapped sugar canes and fruit drops. The sourness in his system settles in his cheeks, bloating, inflaming them, and his eyes narrow and his mouth opens in anticipation of violence or a satisfactory answer. But just then, in the nick of time, his associates call him from the sidewalk. Stone faced men in camel's hair coats and brown hats pacing along a row of black Cadillacs. Exhausts smoking, wipers tick tocking. A few men dust the newly fallen snow off the front and rear windows. Coattails flying, hands battening down hat brims against the sudden high winds. Ditching and stomping cigarettes in the patches of dirt around the barren trees. I see all this through Johnny's bay window. He's distracted from his fury by my gaze, follows it and sees a crony making the Italian hand signal for *What the fuck's going on, are you crazy?* four fingers crowded around thumb, limp wrist bobbing up and down like our grandmothers used to pray. Johnny waves the wave of dismissal, arm swift along the horizon and then down, slamming the sun beneath the ocean. The hulking men climb in, and the caravan of Caddies makes it way slowly across the bay window.

"The scene, Johnny, the scene just now," I say with excitement, "is straight out of *La Bohème* where Rodolpho's friends call him to go to the Caffè Momus and he sings in a lyric strain reflecting the love affair that has just begun that he'll meet his friends at the café later on, he's not alone, there are two, he and a young, beautiful seamstress named Mimi who lost her way in the dark, her candle having gone out on the staircase, and so she can't find her keys, and knocked at their garret door for a light."

"Fuck Puccini!" Johnny roars. "And fuck Rodolpho and fuck Mimi!"

"But isn't it wonderful how our beloved operas continue to speak to us?"

"Look," he snaps, leaning forward, "you're wasting my time. I want the whys and wherefores of your fucken tears and now!" He tugs at his left trousers, exposing the .25 strapped to his ankle.

I spring from the couch crying, gasping, trembling. Throw myself on the floor beside his chair, bow my head and reach up blindly with outstretched arms.

Johnny's granite arms enfold me, clasp me to his chest cushioned beneath the banlon by an excelsior of silvering hair. He places a warm hand on my cheek, then guides it to his, which is running with tears. "The women in the neighborhood," he chokes, "ran away when they saw your carriage..."

"Not all of them, Johnny, not all of them. The women shopping in the shadows beneath the el, they waited for me. In front of Termini's bread store, Arturo's photography studio, Mrs. Palermo's grocery store. They gathered around the carriage, and my mother proudly stepped aside. These women looked down at me, smiling, tears flowing. They said that in their entire lifetime they had never seen such beautiful eyes. In their entire lifetime they had never seen such long curly lashes. 'Blink your eyes one last time,' they tittered. 'We will never again see such beautiful eyes, such beautiful lashes.'"

"And you did!" Johnny exults, his voice cracking. "You stopped crying and blinked and blinked your eyes for them! Your screams cleared the way for a lifelong image, a pair of beautiful eyes shining in the center of a hard life."

"You are a poet, Johnny."

"Oh, he goes on," his voice lilting, "no matter what those women were doing, day or night, they put it aside and made pilgrimages to your house in order to rock you, sing to you..."

"Nee na naw na..." we intone our first lullaby, rocking to and fro in unison.

"My grandmother who lived around the corner needed me," I murmur.

"You couldn't walk so you screamed for her..."

"As my father walked me through the bathroom, I forced my screams so they'd carry across the backyards. Into her back window, her bedroom where she prayed to the scene of Calvary above her bed. She heard my summons. She dismissed her husband's objections with a swift wave of her arm. Her grandson, her first born, needed her to sleep. This tiny woman, toothless, black hairs sprouting from her facial moles, she walked into the night alone, into her freedom, uphill under the stars to the corner of Seventy fourth Street, right on Sixteenth Avenue, then down through a sea of leaves in the fall, around our garden of honeysuckle vines and snowballs in the summertime, always up the brick steps, through the great white steel door with her key, up the green stairs, and she took me in her sweet, smelly, soft, fetid arms onto the rocking chair and then back and forth, back and forth, singing.

Johnny sucks up his tears. The sadness in his face crosses to an endearing smile. "I gotta tell ya dis. I heard it from Sam da baba, you know, Sam's, next ta da florist's..."

"Yeah..."

"Your fadda walks in and sits don as if fa a haircut on one a doze wiah chairs and he's cryin. He's gonna tro himself out da window, he says, because his son's been cryin eighteen owuz a day fa five yees. Sam knows he ain't gonna do dis and keeps snippin. But the guys in da corna crowded ova da scratch sheet they just know a grownup guy in a white gown is cryin in da baba shop. They snikka like da morons we ah. Sam has to shut da idiots up. Dennists, he tells em, wear their white gowns outta da office, too, on their way ta lunch or up da cawna to da baba shop. And this dennist happens to be a good honest man, Sam says, he married a neighborhood girl outta duty. And he built a family, Sam adds. He had a planned daughta--Marietta, he called her after seein da operedda."

"I was in the kitchen when Marietta came home. I stopped crying..."

"You were five years old and could walk..."

"See, too, and think..."

"You looked down the narrow hallway to the entrance to your mother's bedroom..."

"She sat in a plain chair, breasts free, Marietta in her arms. Serious look..."

"She knew you were watching her..."

And then Johnny and I, arms spread, heads turned up to the chandelier, our voices soar together: "*And da sista waz in da mudda's ahms, and da mudda, da Atalian mudda, da foist woman, finally moved on ta somebody else...*"

Animal Magnetism

"Do you think, Johnny, that Marilyn Monroe was attracted to Joe D. the man? Or Ava Gardner, Gloria Vanderbilt, Linda Christian, Mia Farrow, to the humanness of Frank Sinatra?

"Note that after her marriage to Frank, Ava Gardner had an affair with the matador Dominguin. Such was the depth of her love for the bull and its trappings, she moved to Madrid, in fact died there. She had always loved the bull. While she was with Frank, she loved the bull. *Frank* was a bull. A bull with a beautiful baritone voice.

"Especially non--Italian women are drawn to the animal in us. Somehow they sense it, can smell it, even from afar. My girlfriend smelled it from across the ballroom floor. Let's face it, Johnny, all of us, we *are* animals.

"There's Jake the Bull, Sly the Stallion. Each and every one of us is a fox. But the winds may be changing. Stallone has a script on his desk about the life of Giacomo Puccini. That's right, our beloved Puccini, composer of the all time favorites, *La Bohème* and *Madame Butterfly*. Puccini, you should know, raped his maidservant who then went mad. The family brought suit. The King of Melody was acquitted. His favorite sport was shooting birds and fowl. His Madame Butterfly, *Cio cio San*, wasn't attracted solely to Pinkerton's flashy uniform."

"Me? I'm an animal, too. I'm several animals in one. First and foremost I'm a chimp."

"No, not chump, chimp."

Lefty likes gorillas, adores chimps. At least once a month she goes to the Bronx Zoo and lingers for hours around the cages, feeding the chimps bananas so as to animate their hands, her favorite part.

"Ever watch a monkey peel a banana?" Lefty asked me last Saturday night.

"Just like a human, I imagine," the chimp answered.

Lefty loves *my* hands, too. I was telling her about the origin of mosaic art, how centuries ago Italian cave dwellers only had pebbles to make art, suddenly, Lefty took my hands and pressed them against her breasts. "I love your hands on me," she sighed.

"You love just my hands?" groped the chimp.

"Your eyes most of all," Lefty said, confirming what I had always thought, that a monkey's eyes are its salient human feature: endearing, vulnerable, childlike.

I guided her thin body to my lap, threw back my head and opened my eyes wide. Her eyes, her crossed eyes, approached mine.

"What color are my eyes now?" the chimp implored, gazing with joyous expectation at the tree rich with foliage outside his window.

"Green. Sometimes they're blue. Gray, hazel. It's uncanny how they change color."

The chimp was wise enough to leave the deep meaning of his eyes' changing color to his master.

Lefty told the chimp what he wanted to hear the following evening. She called on Sunday around eight instead of her daily seven, after a long day going antiquing with her husband. Sometimes he places his arm around her, Lefty told me. "And I respond." She surrenders her head to the warmth, the comfort of her husband's cradle. Over the phone she said, "Your cock is beautiful. I think of it every night before I go to sleep, and I think of it every morning on awakening." Her telephone is in her study, which is adjacent to her bedroom. Beyond the bedroom sprawl three spacious rooms around which she traipses décolleté, and she sleeps naked beside her husband. My cock hovers above their bed. It's there for her in her dreams and in the early morning sunlight. Her husband sees its effects on her face, the happiness, the serenity. One night, I fear, attracted by the blossoming of her womanhood, the woman emerging from the child, he'll turn over to her.

I'm also a horse.

After her discourse on the chameleon nature of my eyes, Lefty, still sitting in my lap, instructed, "Make me wet."

The chimp's hands, fingers, lips, tongue, all worked up a prodigious lather. Lefty bolted from the yellow club chair, eyes darting wildly. "Get in bed. I must have you inside me."

I hurried to the bed, shedding clothes. Lay on my

back, propped my head on pillows so that I could see her face driving, then go giddy with pleasure, see the saliva through her teeth.

She mounted. Her left hand facilely guided me in. Her fingers are long, bony. Her palms, perfect, moon like. Her hands are those of a beautiful queen. Not a beautiful queen in the ordinary sense, like Elizabeth, but a beautiful cross eyed, left handed queen, with chicken legs and deep chestnut hair that only sunlight can fathom, and with teeth that are bucked, gapped. Harnessing the extent of me, she rode and bucked and rode and bucked.

"You're so big! So deep inside me!"

"And this when I've already come," pronounced the chimp.

Trotting to the bathroom, I looked down and saw that my cock was that of a horse. Cantilevers were needed

109

to hold it up, carry it along. "Ever see a horse with a hardon,
Johnny? Tremendous!"

My ship had made a short stopover in Madeira, and I
was on my way to the linen markets to buy my mother
tablecloths, accompanied by an operatic coach, Tony, and
Tony said, "Look there!" On the other side of the square,
standing perfectly still and broadside to me, was a horse, and
this horse had a hardon that ran the entire length of the
underbelly, from hind legs to fore. Thick as a giant Genoa
soppressata.

I've always been a horse. Any time my mother
desired, she could transform me to a horse. If a neighbor
had something heavy to carry down to the garage, a
refrigerator, my mother would say, "Oh, Mrs. Ernesto, don't
you bother, my son will carry it, he's a horse."

Instead of kissing me, even a peck on the cheek, my

mother demonstrated her profound love for me by punching my arm. Her best shot, biting her tongue, flush on the bicep. Kissing and other disgusting displays of affection were for strangers like my girlfriend at that time, an Argentine lady. Wild signoritas could do anything they wanted with me but only she, my mother, truly loved me. She could punch me because she knew that she was the source of all my power and that I had the strength, patience and resilience of a horse. I'd neigh, snuggle up against her mammoth arm, hoist a hock onto her thick shoulder.

"How was maternal love first manifested to you, Johnny?"

I'm an elephant. I have the testicles of an elephant.

Whenever I told my Argentine compañero that I wasn't Italian, I was really American, she'd guffaw, "Yeah, sure," and then she'd make a circle with her forefingers and thumbs, leaving a little space between the thumbs to indicate that the circumference was infinite. The same hand sign the old opera loving members of our families made after Caruso or Tebaldi finished an aria. The sign translates to: "He (or she) has the balls of an elephant." That is, they sang with such heart, such courage that they had to be more than human; in fact, they're elephants. What better way to describe the grandeur of a species than by the size of its testicles.

I'm a steer. A steer in the calf roping event at the rodeo.

Saturday night before Lefty rode me, before I lay on my back propped up by pillows, she licked her lips. This is her call for some appendage in her mouth. The look on her face now is distant, desperate, nerves and blood vessels rush to her mouth, elongating it, arouse insatiable hunger in it, and like a lioness stalking a herd from the bush, with the tip of her tongue she slowly, methodically circles and moistens every inch of her lips. I placed four fingers in her mouth. She sucked, compressed them, but in time I had to withdraw them or else I'd become the one fingered chimp. I sat at the edge of the bed, legs apart. Lefty dove. I had bought a red floor mat and placed it alongside the bed to cushion her knees. While she had me in her mouth, I reached out with my arms to cup her head, soothe her arms. She slapped my hand away. Then it happened, and it happened so fast and with such deft sleight of hand that I was unable to resist. With her free hand, her right, and all in one fluid motion, she untied the ribbon in her hair and wrapped the ribbon several times around my wrists. There was, of course, no knot, and the chimp had the strength to free himself, but he stayed manacled a while, believing he was amused.

"We're all animals, Johnny, except you. You're plain ole Johnny, a name wholly unto yourself. Your impeccable reputation has something to do with it. You married an Italian girl and stayed in the neighborhood. Wherever you go, your wife and mother make you whole. Make you home. Occasional outings to lower Manhattan don't amount to leaving home. Your place of business is in lower Manhattan. You like to stroll, eat there. And I'm not going to ask you if you've had your share of non Italian bimbos. You're simply Johnny. The boy next door.

"There was a woman who lived not exactly next door to us but about a block away, in a tenement adjacent to the el. Every morning at sunrise and every evening at dusk she threw open her window and screamed, 'Jahnneee! Jahnneee!' Her daily scream accompanied by the roar of the train came through my bedroom window. After hearing the woman for years, one day I asked my mother about her.

"'She's crazy,' my mother said.

"I didn't imagine that the woman was calling a brother or husband. She was calling her son. She called him in the morning, as he had stayed out all night. At dust, dinnertime, she called him in from his play, the way all our mothers called us at that time.

"Are you him, Johnny? Are you my neighbor I never saw, the boy who was lost?"

Images of a Lifetime

She sits on a bench in a railway station, staring across the tracks, her field of vision broken every half hour or so by an incoming train. Now she stares at a huge wheel, occasionally her eyes lift slowly up to a window, and the whistle sounds distant, three thousand miles away. Her skin and her coat and her hair, which has grown down to her seat and over the back of the bench, are white, all with a hint of pink. The vestiges of her youthful beauty and charm are her nose, still aquiline, the bone holding its slope and point, and her shoes, slight and open, fastened with buckles, revealing short socks fringed with lace turned yellow. The chatter of boarding and departing passengers and their groups is indecipherable.

A young railwayman approaches her, holding a sandwich and a piece of fruit. "My grandfather and my father preceded me on this railroad," the handsome railwayman says to her, "and they told me your name is Lily and your coat is red and your hair is blonde, and you've been sitting on this bench day and night and throughout the seasons of fifty one years." He holds out food to her.

The corners of her foam slaked lips descend slightly, and she exhales a stream of air which on hitting the gray cold smokes and billows. "I'm waiting for a train," she says sharply, "a special train, one from Brooklyn carrying my fiancé back to me, my Willie."

Willie's blue jacket hangs on the back of a straight chair. His white shirtsleeves are rolled up. He tosses the last of his things into a vinyl suitcase resting on a white cotton coverlet. His black hair and blue eyes are wild. He's in a hurry. It's five o'clock, and his train leaves Penn Station at eight. His father wearing a worn burnt sienna hat stands in the doorway, looking at photographs. He reviews them several times. "She has blonde hair," he says in Neapolitan, as if his stare and repetition and foreign pronouncement will change the color of the woman's hair from blonde to brown. "I saw blondes in Sicily, Sicilian blondes," the old man says. "Refuse of the Norsemen. Here in Bensonhurst I don't see a blonde in thirty years. God bless America."

Willie smiles, beams. "She's not a Norseman, pa. She's a native of Halifax, and yes, she has blonde hair and she's beautiful, too. As soon as I get back, we're going to marry."

"Halif…" the old man tries.

"Halifax. Halifax. The capital of Nova Scotia. Where I've been doing post graduate work. Where all the salmon comes from."

"Ah, salmon," the old man sighs, and just now a third figure enters the image, a boyhood friend, Slim. The old man leaves because Slim is Sicilian and as a matter of course became a button. Testing whether his old friend's ear for language has changed during his years up in Halifax, Slim boasts in aggravated Brooklyn English, "I just come from bustin the kneecaps with a Louisville slugger of a Greek art dealer sellin the boys Italian Impressionist paintings for tree tousand a picture and then on a tour of the old country Johnny Bath Beach sees the same paintings for tree dollars." This would not be enough to break the man's legs, Slim explains, just get back the money and a percentage of sales, but on top of everything the swindler was fooling around with one of the boys' wives in the back of the shop. "You know," Slim says, "where they frame the pictures." A friendly, talkative customer saw them hiding back there, and

this would have been enough to ice the bastard, but at the sit
down the Don decided that the cuckold was not really one
of the boys, he was their dentist. And besides, the Don said,
his wife's too young for him, a real dish. "You know, Willie,
you could get a job with this dennist."

"I do a lot of skating now," Willie muses. "Lily and
I, we ice skate together. I'm going back to marry her, and
then I'm going to set up an office in one of the barracks of
the Citadel."

"The Citadel?" Slim says.

"The fort crowning the hill on which Halifax is
built," Willie says, sounding a little funny. "It overlooks
Bedford Basin, a magnificent sheet of water, and Lily and I
are going to build a house on the slope of the hill. We met
up at the fort, she was on tour with her college and I heard
that the Citadel was garrisoned by Canadian troops and was

curious, went up there expecting to see those Canadian Mounties. You know, all in brown, pork pie hats tied tight under the chin, whistles in their mouths. But they turned out to be regular guys, and have teeth, too. Teeth are teeth, Slim. I really have to go now. My train leaves at eight."

"You have to eat, don't you? Come to my house for dinner. Everybody wants to see you."

Willie hesitates.

Slim says, "I'll tell you what: I'll *drive* you to Penn Station."

Slim carries the vinyl suitcase, and Willie runs his left hand along the steel banister his father fashioned with his hands in his cellar. A twin banister so that the people next door have something to hold. Two smooth, solid rods shining even more brightly tonight, kissed by the moonlight.

Silver bullets frozen and materialized into metallic spirals every inch of their journey, the eternal target the sidewalk.

The friends bound onto the sidewalk, coattails flying, and as they hustle up the block, Willie looks up at the black night filled with stars. He heard that it takes millions of years for the light of one star to reach the eyes, but he likes to think that the stars are really there, shining now. He blinks his eyes and a hurt look comes over his face, a mixture of bewilderment and tenderness, the product of straining wildly to glimpse his loved one and the person in the way is slapping his face.

Slim flips the latch of the black iron gate outside his house. Up five steps and the outer door is open. The sun porch is cool. They pass through an inner door, and immediately at the right, standing at the foot of the stairs leading up to the bedrooms, is a grandfather's clock. You could see the long, bronze pendulum swinging, hear the ticking. "It's slow an hour," Slim whispers. "We put it back because my father insists on eating at six and my sister Gertie likes to go out after work. The old man never knows."

Willie sits in a chair at the dining room table, crouching low, his spine collapsed. The power of his shoulders and arms cannot lift him up. His suit holds a gray hue, and his carnation is white. He's thick and bald. His blue eyes are always watered from blinking open and shut day and night and throughout the seasons of fifty one years. When he opens his eyes, he expects to see Slim. He sees dark, heavy faces with bulbous noses, low foreheads, black hair and hidden eyes. He doesn't know where his suitcase is. He's on a train sitting at a window beside a friendly stranger.

He sees a multitude of silver and glasses of all shapes and dishes shuttled in and out of the kitchen by young hands and then old ones, always coarse, always red. He sees the sunrise over Bedford Basin. The crystal chandelier fills the room with sheer white light, and the heavy curtains are drawn. The train flies north through New Hampshire, Maine, past sleepy farmhouses and silhouetted mountains. He sneezes, mechanically raises himself enough to withdraw a damp, yellow handkerchief from his back pocket. The conductor calls, "Halifax Station!" He's handed a fresh handkerchief, blows his nose grown bulbous. The grandfather's clock chimes on the quarter hour. He looks at his Hamilton watch and doesn't understand the time. He sees a sweet, a favorite, loose and yellow, coconut custard pie. He's given a piece, nibbles at a morsel.

The hidden eyes turn toward the doorway. "Oh,

here's Gertie. Just in time, Gertie. Sit down," and he closes his eyes and sees Gertie dressed for springtime in a V neck silk shirt covered with petals, white pleated skirt, white stockings. She sits down and eats fast, catching up. The steak knife slices through her forefinger, and the blood gushes and arcs toward the chandelier. "Look," Gertie says nonchalantly, "blood." Out of pity he takes her out, for a walk, holding her arm, wrapped finger held aloft. It heals and he takes her out again. Then, in the infinite darkness of his closed eyes, a young man in a dark suit and white shirt walks into the dining room at full pace and, ignoring the reproving glances, goes up behind his father, taps his arm, leans down to an ear. "Let's go, champ. I have your suitcase. We have a train to catch."

A Gourmet Dish of Pasta

Johnny leans forward and with sure hands picks up a piece of paper, a yellow piece of paper, from the coffee table. "I just don't understand," he says, shaking his head. "This is the announcement for the reading in Hoboken. What was the theme?"

"I'm sorry, I forget."

"'From the Old Country to the New Neighborhood,' it says here, and you go and read about a Jew..."

"There were Jews in the old neighborhood."

"Yeah, up on Twentieth Avenue, out by Flatbush, but did they come near the el? They wouldn't come within earshot of our fucken train. You never saw a Jew, let alone play with one."

"You forget, John, Jews settled Boro Park, the next

neighborhood from Bensonhurst going toward the city. I saw Hasidic Jews on the train all the time; they sat there reading their holy books and didn't care who was watching or what we thought. Admirable, I'd say."

"You didn't read about no Hasidic Jew..."

"Do you remember our first introduction to racism? What our grandparents, and then our parents, used to say in the kitchen all the time, around the dinner table. They called Jews and Blacks by the same name. 'Schfazzas,' and the Jews got all the jobs, the Jews keep the Italians down, the Jews help one another while we don't. Why, our ancestors asked, don't we help one another? And the question never went answered. I remembered how Jews and Blacks are depicted in our films. In *Mean Streets*, Charlie played by Harvey Keitel, a Jew, he sees a woman sitting at the end of the bar and says to Tony, 'Who's that girl?' 'Jewish,' Tony says. 'How do you know?' asks Charlie/Harvey. 'Look at her,' Tony says. Charlie: 'She don't look Jewish.' Tony: 'She comes in here every night with a different guy, you know how they are.'"

"That's reality," Johnny says.

"In *The Godfather*," I go on, "at the sitdown of the Heads of Five Families about drugs, Don Stracci stands up and says, 'In my city we would keep the traffic in the dark people. They're animals anyway, so let them lose their souls.' Then we object to Spike Lee's responses and to Leonard Jeffries', that City University professor who said at a conference that there's a conspiracy to put down and keep Blacks out of the movies, programmed by people with names like Greenberg and Vigliano. Lee, Greenberg, Jeffries, Vigliano, they go to the movies. The young animals in Bensonhurst go to the movies. Yousef Hawkins went to the movies. I remembered the poet warrior Ugo Foscolo,

Garibaldi's favorite. Young Foscolo led his gang in an uprising to free the Jews penned up in his neighborhood of Xante, an isle off Venice. Jews were arrested if seen talking to a Christian, the lights in their neighborhoods were shut off so they couldn't stroll, convene, chat of an evening. I remembered Dumas and Garibaldi, the Novelist and the Lion, the Black Frenchman and the Red Italian. They were friends, comrades in arms, fought together in Sicily..."

"No kidding..."

"That's right, and so I thought that since I'd be reading after the kid professor, I'd provide some lighthearted relief, a playful intermezzo of sorts. The Jew I read about has delighted children around the world for generations, grew up with Italians in Chicago, works in our cafes now, and do you know what he asked me once on Bleecker Street? This genius, this millionaire, he collars me and says,

'Nicholas, where can I get a gourmet dish of pasta?' I looked around, the sun was shining, Bobby Fontana was across the street, vending. 'I'll get back to you,' I said, and then went directly to Tutta Pasta on Carmine Street and to Raffetto's on Houston Street, where they make fresh every day, and inquired about the restaurants they supply. But in the end I knew that my friend's gourmet dish of pasta lay in the palm of my hand. I called him. 'Come over,' I said. 'I'm making pasta tonight.'"

Autobiography

"So, Johnny, poste haste I send the kid professor my autobiography. Right away he calls me. 'Sir,' he begins, softening me up, 'I didn't ask for your autobiography in a hundred words or less. This took me about two minutes to read. And there's nothing here about you. Just a couple of images of this Lily and Willie.'

"'Look, kid,' I say, 'the world doesn't want to know about me. It wants to know about Johnny.'

"'Yes,' he says cautiously, 'the world does want to know about Johnny. Three quarters of the world. The other one quarter wants to know about you. Which adds up to fifty billion people. You and me and everybody else,' he gets testy, 'know full well that Johnny isn't about to talk about his private life. He's like Joe D. Ever hear Joe talk about

131

Marilyn?'

"'Sicilians are like that,' I remind him.

"'Not you!' he screams. 'You're one Sicilian who'll talk and write about anything and everything. At least you have in the past. Come on! Every day for the past twenty years practically every word you've uttered and written breaks our sacred code of *omerta*.'

"Here, Johnny, I get a little hurt, a little sad. I told the kid I was sorry, but then I thought that maybe there's not much difference between silence and a tremendous raucous. When you see the A bomb exploding on Hiroshima, don't you feel a terrible silence about it all? So I say to the kid with some remorse, 'Joe D.'s silence speaks of a great deal. In it you feel his love for her. You see his unspoken love in the elegant way he's progressing through his life, in our memory of his silent action of laying roses on her grave.

Every Saturday night I give my girlfriend a jewel. Who cares? I'm just your average Italian Joe.'

"'Average for us, maybe,' the kid gets his *Calabrese* up, 'but our average translates to everybody's else's spectacular. Each one of us is part D'Annunzio, part Capone. You're *all* D'Annunzio. Have you ever had a job, a boss? You don't even have health insurance. Love is all you care to do. You know, I read every poem D'Annunzio wrote but never knew until you told me that he concocted his own perfume.'

"'I don't use perfume. I don't use deodorants either,' I say to get the kid off.

"'Have you ever received a complaint?' he asks me.

"'Quite to the contrary,' I say. 'My natural odors appear to engender enthusiasm. I remember an enthusiastic American girl, Claire something, she said I smelled like the sea. 'You're my Sinbad the Sailor,' she told me. I told her I had never been on a boat, was raised on concrete, in the shadows of the el. She laughed, and I saw in her open mouth that her teeth were cracked, abscessed, on some the roots had died and these teeth were black. 'My father's a dentist,' I confessed, 'I'll take you to him.' She laughed even harder, a terrible sight. 'Then you're my Sinbad the Dentist!' she guffawed. Funny, women are, aren't they?"

"'Things like this should go in your autobiography.' The kid's spirit, I have to admit, was indomitable. 'Don't you see,' he goes on.

"'No...'

"'Look, you don't use deodorants, right? And women of all ages and types keep breaking down your door, right? I'll bet you a dinner at Vesuvio's that for any two women you don't smell the same. You're natural, and the more you're natural, the more you're different. You're the

Italian chameleon. You're like smoke. Women can't put their finger on you. Ever see smoke billow the same way twice? You're greater than Leonardo da Vinci--'

"'Come on, kid...'

"'Da Vinci invented paint but used it himself. You invented Italian smell but you don't use it. Only others use it. You yourself probably don't know your own smell. Weren't you the one who told me that while they're performing, opera singers can't hear their own voices, that even Caruso and Tebaldi didn't know how they really sounded, that the golden, angelic timbres of their voices were at the disposal and pleasure of others? Well, your *smell* is at the disposal and pleasure of others. Precisely the myriad forms that pleasure has taken is five hundred pages right there. I'm sorry, but I'm sending these paltry pages back to you.'

"'No, kid, please,' I implore him. I didn't want to see those images again, Johnny. 'For a while,' I tell him, 'work on the other Italians' autobiographies. Let's just say I had a bad morning. I'll give the whole matter further thought and get back to you. I promise.'"

Our Child

She sits in the yellow club chair. Her bare feet, fallen arches, rest flat on the red floor.

I tore up the gray, stained rug and painted the wooden floorboards deck red. I wanted to see the color of her hair, her lipstick and her fingernails when she's alone in her study, when she sleeps naked beside her husband.

I pull up a folding chair, lift her legs onto my lap and begin to massage her feet. They hurt after her long walks in the afternoon, she told me. I felt the pain of her steps.

We do not say the word but we know. Her breasts have swelled. Her nipples ache. Her face is aglow. She's going to the doctor next week.

"I'm prepared to marry you," I say. "Get a place and raise our child. I love you."

She gasps, a sudden pain.

"Whatever decision you make, I support," I go on. "Whatever decision you make is right."

"Whatever decision I make is wrong," she says. "My life is ruined."

"If you're referring to your marriage, you have none," I say.

The pain hits again, stronger this time. She throws back her head, clasps her stomach.

We prepared for this.

I had bought her flowers and she carried them to the restaurant, the Village Tavern. She had the waiter place the flowers in a vase, which he set on our table.

"Have you ever been married?" I asked at some point.

"I *am* married," she answered. "Sort of," she added.

"There's no passion."

I wondered if I could satisfy that way a woman twenty years younger than I.

Three nights later, after an elegant dinner here, I came up behind her to kiss her red hair. She turned, her eyes closed, her lips parted. The following Monday we moved to my single bed, the moment arrived and I paused, rose up and showed her a condom.

"Forget those," she said. "I have an IUD."

I tossed the condom to the red floor.

Marriage and romance do not go together, she's said many times. Writing is the most important thing in her life. She's ambitious, she admitted. Her husband pays the bills.

I've said that I reached a point in my life where I want to begin a new cycle, marry a woman I love and have children. Instead of waking up with memory of my dreams,

I wake up with the names of our children. "Jules and Primavera," I told her.

She laughed, but one Saturday night while preparing our salad, she said, "In the Jewish tradition, children are named for the dead."

"A wonderful tradition," I remarked.

"For grandparents who have died," she continued.

"What were your grandparents' names?" I asked.

"Anna and Benjamin," she said.

"Beautiful names," I said.

I press my thumbs into the soles of her feet. "Our children will be beautiful," I say.

She doubles over from the pain. Begins to sob.

I pick her up. I stand in the middle of the room, one arm around her shoulders, one arm under her legs. I feel a wetness on my arm. "Oh, no..." I sigh. The wetness spreads, thickens. One leg slips from my grasp. "Oh, no..."

Our child, blood, flesh and water, drops onto the red floor.

Funny Writers

The neurologist is all smiles this morning. "No permanent deficits," she reassures me. "Most likely a few bouts of vertigo down the road but they pass." She writes in my chart chained to my bedpost.

"Please read to me," I scribble in my all purpose pad.

Dr. Bennet is wall eyed and she yodels.

"1/20/90. Bleeding from both nostrils, vomited quantity of old blood. Mental condition…"

Gay walks in, holding a hat box. His preliminary investigation found that after the station wagon ran the light and crashed into me and I was tumbling through the air, my hat flew off and rolled like a wheel across the junction of Bleecker and LaGuardia Streets, but then got lost in the traffic up toward the park.

"You'll have to wait outside," Dr. Bennet yodels with some derision, not knowing who Gay is, that he's the top Italian banana. Gay doesn't move, he stares at me, and Dr. Bennet eyes him up and down. She also doesn't know that Gay is the ubiquitous Italian Adolph Menjou, dressing up morning, noon, as well as night in his bathroom, tennis court, in his bedroom. Dr. Bennet turns to me for corroboration. She wants Gay outside. She wants me all to herself. I nod and blink my eyes as a way of pleading for my friend to stay. Blood commingles with my tears.

"What's wrong with his eyes?" Gay asks.

"Ecchymosis of both upper eyelids. It's nothing."

The social worker pokes her head in the doorway. She's smiling. "By the way," she says, looking down at her clipboard, "I agree with what your mother told you. You *should* have some nice friends." Last night I scribbled that my mother used to tell me that I should have some nice friends.

Gay unties the pretty red ribbon on the hat box, takes out a black Stetson and places it loosely on my head. "Now he could walk down a street and everybody would recognize him." Gay steps back, a smile tugging at his taut lips.

Except for my eyes, nose and ears, my head is bandaged, and my right arm and left leg are in casts, the left leg suspended in traction. It looks like I'm forever bracing myself after a long fall. I'm frozen inches before the big splash. My jaw is wired and so Gay, the Italian Horace Greeley, has to rely on the neurologist for his information. "What happened?"

Dr. Bennet yodels, "Just a moment, I took down a History." She fishes for my file in her thick, black briefcase.

The barber, an old timer, stops by on his morning rounds. His smile is sweet, faraway. He's wearing a white gown and holds a small, black satchel. He's a hybrid between a doctor and a dentist. "You may not remember now," he says with a beautiful voice, mellifluous baritone, "but I gave you your first haircut and even then told you that you were so handsome that one day you would become a movie star." Then he follows the social worker down the hall.

Dr. Bennet, yodeling: "Here it is...History.

"On evening before admission, patient purchased grapes at Grand Union, and at first was disappointed, he states, because he missed the three consecutive nights of a sale on cantaloupes, 99 cents each. He says Grand Union is further east than he normally ventures, indicating he may be on the threshold of a new life in a different locale. But he's happy, smiling, looking up at the sky as he walks out between two parked cars against the light. He follows the pedestrian ahead of him, 'instilling trust' in him. With one hand patient holds a brown paper bag filled with grapes and with the other tosses the grapes up into the air. He's thinking of his tootsie. His term: 'tootsie.' Then he nonchalantly turns and looks down and, at the point of impact, captures the station wagon's right fender on his left leg. 'Fixes' on the fender, he elaborates, 'glinting in the light of the corner streetlamp.' He hears a boom and after that remembers nothing."

Dr. Bennet looks up and away somewhere. "He was knocked out."

Gay, in all earnestness: "The book starts here, with the accident, and then you go back and tell the love story."

Between spread legs, in a line of vision inches above

my extended crotch, I see Kurt's silly ole face in the doorway. He's pinching his nose, snorting, stifling uncontrollable laughter. Kurt is fond of saying that all he has to do is look at my face and he laughs. My face could reflect the loss of the love of my life and Kurt looks at it and laughs. I think Kurt is funny. I think it's funny how he met his last wife. Insidious gossip circulated by a mutual friend, Professor Ralph Stiller, funny nonetheless. Kurt goes into a toilet to pee. Some fund raiser, awards ceremony and Kurt has to go. She's hiding in a stall, taking her chances. Peeking out. Kurt has his zipper down, pecker out, one stance a man dreads will be interrupted, a position he guards with his life from the time he can stand up himself, until the day he dies. She tiptoes out, scurries up, introduces herself.

Outside my hospital room, Kurt doubles over from laughter, falls down. The corridor out there is familiar to him. He's paced it many long, silent nights. Psychiatric is down the hall. Writers like to walk, and St. Vincent's Psychiatric is just a cigarette away from Kurt's writing studio. "Please, my back!" he cries, holding his sides. "I just fell off a horse!"

Gay goes out and helps his colleague up. They approach the bed, one short, the other tall. One dressed like a slob, the other like Adolph Menjou. One finds everything funny, the other nothing funny. They have in common that they're aging writers. They have in common that they're my friends. Kurt drools, "He'll walk into class with a tourniquet wrapped around his chin and grit that he has such a terrific toothache that he can't speak, the students should just write a story."

Dr. Bennet and Gay are silent. Kurt's face goes serious, and I try to smile at the way the loose skin of his perennial smile collapses, like a hound's. Suddenly, Kurt breaks from the others and pushes forward until his face is inches from mine. "It hurt?" he says with the voice and accent of a brilliant boy. I nod. "What's this?" he says upbeat again, picking up the all-purpose pad and colored markers on my chest.

"Sometimes he scribbles when he's conscious," Dr. Bennet yodels.

"Look at this, Gay! Each word a different color!"

"I'd like to see that." Gay with some enthusiasm, and he sidles up.

My friends are close to me, press lightly against my arm. Each holds a side of the pad. "Shall we?" Gay says. "Oh, let's," Kurt responds. One an alto, the other a bass, they read with one beautiful voice:

"Men smack him, throw him to the ground, inject

him with phenobarbital. Women bang his outstretched hands with a wooden spoon, blackboard pointer, pull his hair at the temples. The boy is three years old, away at a school near an ocean. For the next fifty years a daydream plays over and over on a plateau of silence that stretches from the tip of his toes to the top of his head. A woman has come for him. She has come to reach the top of the hill, the fence up there. Her face is large, big boned, shadowy plains. It resembles his mother's and a South American lover rather late in his life. The woman's skin is dark, and she has black hair that blows in the wind storm sweeping the shore. Her expression is steady, fierce. She kicks aside jagged rocks, thorny bushes that tear at her long dress and her skin, drawing blood. She climbs, strains, pushes upward.

"The boy sits on a blue wooden step. His punishment for not drinking warm milk, for not standing on line to pee. At the start of each day, he goes directly to his punishment, sits down and looks out at the other children playing in the dirt yard. Beyond them is the fence. The boy cannot save himself. Whatever he does for himself is a temporary escape he knows not where to, except it is safer, a quiet plateau where he can rest a while. This plateau was born in the following way.

"The god, the creative touch were the things he loved to do with his mother. He loved to iron straight things: handkerchiefs, towels, sheets. He loved to buff the floor, making it shine after his mother washed it on her knees. He loved to stand beside his mother at the sink, while she filled the basin with water and soap. He went with her to the utility closet in the hall, hard brush and rags. Then she handed him his tools, and he carried them to the landing. He'd begin at the top. The landing and steps are covered with green linoleum bordered by creamy stripes. The stripes have to shine. Pick up dust balls that have a way of accumulating in the corners. The basin is wider than a step almost by half. The boy works his way down on his knees, balancing, scrubbing, drying.

"One fall morning he finds himself at the foot of the staircase. His mother stands on the landing, still, silent, watching. Another woman has her hand on his shoulder. At first, the pressure is slight, and he uses all his strength against it. He grips the deep lacquered banister that at the top and bottom turns at right angles into the wall. The pressure on his shoulder increases. A silence is born, a second, a drop. He's torn from the banister. The silence lengthens, it has ground now and light and space. It is a plateau and the boy springs onto it. From then on, everything falls on this airy, silent plateau. Faces, words,

rain. Everything."

Fascination

We play our first meeting over and over, as if it's a wondrous kind of recorded history, sparkling, elastic, stretching down through all the days we are together. A portion of every time we are together, our eyes shine, our voices quicken as we crystallize images and gestures, recount dialogue, inflate minor characters, dispute with a smile. If we do the same with our second, third, fourth meetings, we have a lifetime together.

"I almost don't go," Lefty says. "I've been depressed for months. I've given up all hope."

"Of what?" I ask.

"Finding romance again."

A light shines in me, the light of our romance.

"I almost don't go, too. I'd never been to Garvin's.

Why go somewhere on Christmas where I don't go during the year?"

We certainly would not go alone.

Lefty went with her friend Nancy, who lived on Bleecker Street. I arranged to meet my friend Joyce at Garvin's.

I hustled up Waverly Place early in compensation for Joyce's trip downtown. Passed the Christmas tree under the Washington Square arch. The perfect tree overwhelmed me with nostalgia, the premature deaths of my mother and father, reduced me to an expectant child on Christmas morning who is always disappointed that his gift is a miniature of the real thing. I did not know the route, the route Lefty and Nancy took to the restaurant. I was unable to retrace Lefty's steps. I did not know whether she passed the tree.

"Do you and your husband celebrate Christmas?" I do not ask her. "Do you buy a tree? I understand you're Jewish, but your husband is an Irish/Italian fellow, was most likely raised Catholic, and every morning saw a tree in his living room."

If Lefty and Nancy did not pass the tree, they circumvented the park and took a southeasterly route. Nancy's idea, which Lefty gladly allowed.

"She copies me. Everything I do she has to do."

Lefty is a fiction writer. One book under her belt. Married. Out for an affair.

Nancy is a poet and university teacher. No books. Married. Out for an affair.

"It's uncanny," I say, "that the entire night I do not see Nancy's face. She's in your group to my left. I glimpse her back. She's tall, isn't she? Long, light hair."

"Nancy is very pretty."

"Where do you two go afterwards?" I ask.

"Soups On. You?"

"Caffè Dante with Joyce."

"I think you and Joyce are together."

"Isn't it awful? I've never seen Joyce with so much makeup. The way she cakes her lips, does up her eyes. I know her boyfriend Tom."

"I feel like an intruder..."

"I know! As soon as we're together, Joyce doesn't leave us alone. I feel like telling her, 'Hey, I like this girl, leave us alone!'"

Nancy was pretty but Lefty didn't feel pretty, yet later on at Soups On, Lefty told Nancy that she'd met someone she liked, while Nancy hadn't.

I kept pulling for Nancy to find a lover so that she'd

be happy like Lefty. "Has Nancy found someone yet?"

"No, but she's looking."

"Has..."

"Not yet."

"Has..."

"Another graduate student."

"Wonderful! How is it?"

"They lock themselves in an office and kiss."

Weeks passed. Nancy and her lover were locked in an office, kissing.

"Have they--"

"They're still kissing."

"Please tell Nancy that if she wishes, she can use my place."

"That's very nice of you but it's over."

A light, in the far left corner of Garvin's restaurant, main ballroom, I needed a light for my cigarette. I'd smoked several already using my own matches, and so I patted my pants pockets, jacket pockets. My head was down somewhere in the direction of lost matches. My eyes were closed, momentarily, I was lost. Suddenly, I sensed an isolated presence in front of me. Some power greater than I, greater than my blood screaming for nicotine. This strange power lifted my head, and my eyes beheld her milling around in one spot five yards in front of me. Her body shimmered to a rock 'n' roll tune.

"You mention rock 'n' roll, remember? In a rare silence, the music gains the foreground, guitar sounds, John Pizzarelli's guitar. The entire night I'm thinking how it is wonderful when a son follows in his father's footsteps with some competence, in this case, in John Pizzarelli's case, and finally I'm able to say to you, 'That's John Pizzarelli, the renowned Bucky Pizzarelli's son,' and you say with a pout, 'At least they could have had some rock 'n' roll.'"

I gestured toward her for a light. The gesture took a lifetime. Left arm raised and curled, hand with cigarette between fore and middle fingers out to her, cigarette fingers slightly spread, gently pointing to a spot somewhere on her torso; at the same time, thick brows raised in endearment, exposing expectant eyes; finally, the head nodded ever so slightly, saying, "Have a match?"

"Nonsense! A light is a pretense for meeting me."

"Yes, if you say so, a pretense but I'm truly searching for a light, I know because Joyce is in my circle in the corner and she's a smoker, has matches, but I can't ask her because also in our corner, within earshot, is that short, fat stockbroker, you know, that ridiculous husband of that ridiculous writing teacher who's always asking me for my methods. This stockbroker who pays the bills, he's against smokers, and so I have to rely on my own resources and then steal a smoke. Then you and I smoke in full glory in front of the ridiculous stockbroker. Funny how we stash that small, glass ashtray on the floor in the corner, tapping our ashes which sometimes hit the mark, sometimes drift and pull apart. The point is, I'm searching for a light."

"You haven't noticed me?" Lefty asks.

"From the moment I take up a position in the corner, I sense the presence of a hat, a black hat, a black porkpie hat. The only hat in the ballroom, I note. After sensing its presence for a solid hour, I feel a vague, distant admiration for the owner. She is a woman, I say to myself, who, despite knowing that she's going to a function full of writers and would be writers, has chosen to wear a hat, and keeps wearing it in the ballroom. She's brazen, courageous, unafraid of calling attention to herself as someone different in a room full of people who believe they are different."

"You think I'm a groupie."

"Writers have groupies, too, you know. Anyway, at first, I sense the hat in a cluster about ten feet and forty five degree angle to my left. A big guy in just a sweater and at least two women form their circle, the hat and a tall, stiff, chic woman, not a writer, Nancy. Bodies are between us, but I keep sensing the hat, it's suspended, floats here and now there, but always close. It doesn't matter what I do or how much time passes, the hat is always there, circling around. Lungs bellow, pressure rises, vessels constrict. I withdraw a cigarette, search for matches and am about to give up hope when the hat, I sense the hat alone, directly in front of me, and it draws up my head. The movement is so easy, so natural, so gay."

She fumbled in her pocketbook, with her left hand, I noticed. She's left handed, I took note. Immediately, I knew that everything was going to be different. Wisps of hair protruded from beneath her hat, sharp curls at the temples, and I saw that her hair was red, copper red living in light. She has red hair, I noted further. Immediately, I knew that everything was going to be strange and wonderful.

"I notice *you* as soon as I walk in," Lefty says.

"Really!"

"That's right, and I know you're an Italian from Brooklyn and also what you look like without clothes."

"Do I like it, you know?"

"Yes, I could tell that, too."

"But how...how can you tell?"

"I just can. I feel like taking you downstairs."

I had checked my coat in the basement where Lefty had it in mind to take me. The line was long, slow. Sprawling behind me, fading into darkness, was Garvin's Latin cabaret. *Open for Fun,* the placard said, *on Thursday and Saturday Nights.* Red, green, yellow spotlights shined on the empty dance floor. I heard the Salsa beat. A huge mahogany horseshoe bar, a gigantic boomerang, concealed just beyond it the lower level of the dance floor. The floor was hard, dark, quiet. Two lively women in uniform had taken my coat. I imagine that Lefty took my hand and guided me across the ballroom, down the stairs. We tested the good cheer of the hatcheck persons, and then had a rollicking good time amid the hundreds of dark, warm shields of wool and cashmere.

"Why don't you say you want to take me downstairs?"

"I've come with Nancy. I should stay with her."

"That is right.   During our first moments we discover that we live only six blocks apart. 'I live near the meat markets,' you say, and I see them, see the warehouses in the dead of night, isolated, ominous, and I offer to walk you home and you say you'll see. But then at the end of the evening you find me again and say, 'I'm going home with my friend. It's been nice to meet you.' You are considerate. You are decent."

She found matches in her pocketbook. She took several stutter steps toward me, tossing the stale air, filling the barren parquet. Her eyes were shining. Her lips were thick, red, parted. I saw the gap in her top front teeth. She held out the open book.

Casa Johnny

Johnny gets up and, for a man his size, five by five, he skirts the coffee table with amazing agility. He has no discernible belly. It's spread evenly over the length and breadth of his body, north, south, east and west. In effect he's one big belly. He's one big belly filled constantly with pasta. This uniform energized belly has a lot to do with his sense of power and his style and grace. It's his armor, his repellent, his freeing up. His pores do not breathe. His skin, hair, nails, all are cemented. At once he's entirely self contained, and the rest of the world, everything and everybody in it, is at bay.

He comes and sits beside me, arm against mine. I feel his weight along the whole extent of the couch. He presses the hollows of my cheeks with his forefinger and thumb. My head is his. All of my intelligence and experience are his. He turns my head but I resist, cannot look into his eyes. Gently, he tips up my chin as if for a kiss, and says, staring at me: "What do you need?"

"A home for aged Italian artists."

"Vinny!" Johnny calls, and Vinny trundles in. He's about the same height and weight as Johnny, but Vinny's hair is not trimmed every afternoon and his eyes are overtly wild. Vinny's belly hangs over his belt. "Catch a plane for Italy tonight, Milan," Johnny tells him. "A hundred years ago, Joe Green donated a million lire to Milan for a home for old singers and musicians. Go to this Casa Verdi and check out how it's administered. Entrance qualifications, stuff like this."

All the while Johnny is addressing Vinny, he's looking at me. Even as he gets up, returns to his wing chair and sits down, Johnny's eyes do not leave mine. I feel free to chime in: "I'd be careful, John, about donating..."

"Shut up! You're fucken sloppy, you know it?" Vinny tucks in his pants. "First of all, what do you mean, *Italian* artists? Italians from Italy, Montreal, Buenos Aires, where?"

"The United States, Johnny."

"All right, then, from here. This I can live with. And what do you mean, *artists*? Performing artists, visual artists...?

"Italo American writers."

"You're so self serving you're disgusting! Why don't you just come out and say you want a place for yourself."

"I wouldn't live in the home, John. I'd destroy it. I've destroyed everything given to me. Cars, houses, clothes, watches, most of all, love."

"All right, all right. But Italo American writers I can house right now in a six room condo."

"By the time the home is built, there'll be more."

"Where do you want this home?"

"In Brooklyn, overlooking the Narrows. The ocean, sea breezes..."

"Vinny, check out Fort Hamilton. They don't need the fort anymore. If that don't work, look into Veteran's Hospital and Dyker Beach golf course. In the last resort, we'll use Appalachia." Vinny turns and leaves. "And no fucken around in Milan. I want the information tomorrow!"

And then Johnny slams the wing of his chair. "Done!" he says, still peering deep into my eyes.

The Last Godfather

Suddenly, about a dozen table lamps go on. The crystal chandelier above the dining room table lights up. It's as if the sun had been reluctant to leave Johnny and me, came down and installed itself in his home. Shading my eyes, I look around for the maid, the butler. There's no one here except Johnny and me. An automatic device was timed to activate the lamps and chandelier with the onset of darkness.

"Well, Johnny," I say with levity, "I'd better be on my way. Thanks a million, but before I go, I'd like to give you a copy of my last book. I inscribed it for you. Signed a personal note from me to you."

My trembling hand reaches into my briefcase and, while my head is bowed, I hear the crack of a firecracker, a bullet. I wince, close my eyes, waiting for it to go straight into my cranium. But I'm still alive when I look up, and see Johnny snap his fingers again. "Alfonso," he says low enough only for us to hear. Still, in walks Alfonso, a huge, hovering, mustached Alfonso, with the eyes and nose of a hawk, weathered skin white with lime, wearing a carpenter's apron strung with appropriate tools except for one, a .38 with silencer. In fingers the size and shape of hammerheads, Alfonso holds a microphone, speakers, roll of electrical wire.

"Johnny, how nice, you've planned some sort of pageant for my benefit."

"Also," Johnny says softly to Alfonso, "block off the ends of the street, use the police barricades in the cellar, and tell everybody on the block to throw open their windows. They're eating now anyway. Anybody in cars, tell them to shut off the motors." Johnny turns to me. "I want to hear what you read at the college in Hoboken."

"Johnny," I choke, "in the book I'm presenting to you, there are twenty different stories. I've read them all over the country, South America, Palermo, too, so when you read them in the privacy of your den, imagine I'm beside you."

His brows raise a fraction of an inch. Instantly, my entire outlook changes.

"You know, after I read in Hoboken, the kid professor came up to me and said, 'I learned something. Hot on hot's no good when I read as well as when I write. When you read,' he said, 'your voice is so soft, your rhythm so easy, natural.'"

Johnny's brows are still raised.

"It will be a great pleasure to read for you, Johnny. I really don't need all this light. See that marble statue behind your lovely snowball plant, that statue of Aphrodite and

Apollo, the brilliant, muted lights around the base, those blues and yellows and greens, they're all the light I need. And please have Mr. Alfonso set up the statue and his mike at the head of the dining room table, I'll read from there. OK?"

Johnny sits back, content. Mr. Alfonso takes care of everything.

I breathe deeply, try to get up. False start. I try again. Suddenly, I'm overcome with a sense of work and duty, and love fills my heart. They conjoin and I move, glide. Adjusting the mike, I say, "The second piece I read in Hoboken, Johnny, was called *The Last Godfather*," and then I read:

The Last Godfather

I am Pippo Napoli Sicilia and I am the last of the great Dons, the last Godfather. After me, after I join Dante in the empyrean, my family of thirty million or so will not need crime to get on, because in their dark souls and untrustful minds I have placed love and beauty and imagination and understanding. Their olive faces will be raised to the Crystalline Heaven. They will be at the point of assimilation into the American race, prepared to ponder the American Revolution and George Washington and Thomas Jefferson and Alexander Hamilton. They will look into one another's eyes and, instead of sensing alarm, will see brother and sister in Faith, Hope and Charity.

For centuries in America, my Italians did not like how they felt about themselves and recognized their displeasure in one another. After pondering this state of affairs for decades, I decided to talk about creativity in general and then, in case I was not understood, to set myself as an example.

People of all sorts, I said, have difficulty writing. You hear a lot, "I can't even write a letter!" and the common explanation is that the empty page or, in the modern age, the empty screen, invokes fear. But the problem is not the emptiness of the page or screen but their position, that is, opposite you, face to face, defiant, adversarial. And so from this moment onward, December 28, 2089, I say to imagine the empty page or screen not directly in front of you but *beside* you. Now in front of you and your companion is the whole of the universe, the sky and the moon and the sun and the heavens.

Then, not waiting to see if I was understood, I set an example.

My last domicile is located on the lower west side of

Manhattan in the building where my mother was born, on the corner of Houston and Sullivan Streets, across from St. Anthony's church. My room is small, a peaceful shrine nine flights up. When you cannot climb any higher, you have reached me. On my sill is a white scalloped bowl replenished each morning with fresh water for the sparrows. High winds blow my geraniums. One flower is wilted, in its demise looks down to the steps of the church. But one flower still faces the heavens, with its last breath bends on its strong thin stem, the flowers rich red, delicate and full.

I am old, 94 years old and, if I can get up, I walk to the river. For the sake of unity, of appearing the same way inside and out, I wear the same clothes: Long johns, terry cloth robe, cotton socks and slippers. On the morning I set the example, Charlie Pino waited outside my door. Charlie owns the bread store on Bleecker Street, but in the morning, in order to pay his daily homage, he leaves his son in the store. Charlie reached up my robe for my right hand, but before it touched his lips and he could say, "Bless you this day, Don Pippo," I grabbed him around the waist and spun him around to a position beside me. Then I said, "Greet me, Charles, while looking at the church, and then let's walk side by side."

I looked everywhere except down at our feet, in front and behind us, across the street, up at the sky. "Not a cloud in the sky today, Charles," I observed.

"Not a single cloud, Godfather," Charlie said.

We came to Father Demo Square on Carmine Street.

"Feed the pigeons today, Charles?"

"Yes, Godfather."

"Day old or fresh?"

"Fresh, Godfather."

"Good, Charles, good. You know, your son's pallor is that of your bread, and his expression of late is bland. It's not good for our sons to do as we do. My son, as you know, is an art historian."

"I'll tell my son to find something else."

"Good. Good."

A block or so from the square, about an hour later, we arrived at York's Ivory Jewelry run by Pretab Kamdar from Bombay, a short, dark, wall-eyed brother. As he approached with an outstretched arm, Charlie advanced and whirled Kamdar around until he was beside us. "Greet the Don from here," said Charlie, and we continued to the river.

Yang the Japanese shoemaker and Bella the female butcher and Juan the Spanish fish vendor and Jake the Jewish pizza maker joined us in the same fashion. Down around West Street I reached into my deep pajama pocket for a wad of cash. "Pass this on to Kamdar," I said, and the money was passed along the line. "Kamdar!" I shouted, "no more killing of elephants for the ivory!"

"No, Godfather, no more."

We fanned out across the highway and looked at the river and the ocean beyond. I led the way to the vicinity of the parking lot about where the Hudson River washes into the Atlantic Ocean. For years I wondered exactly where the fresh water turns to salt. I expressed my wonderment to my family.

"I suppose the scientists have ways of finding out," said Kim, the Korean greengrocer.

Bella, the female butcher, said, "And why do you want to find out, Godfather?"

"I think about the fish," I said, "bass mainly who used to swim between the piers. Where in their desperation do the bass go? If they try a dash to the ocean, do they make the transition to the salt in a safe and healthy way?"

"If the bass die, Godfather," Juan, the Spanish fish vendor, said, "don't you think we'd see them on their bellies on the surface? I don't see any dead bass."

"Neither do I," said Samir, the gay Palestinian restaurateur.

"Neither do I," said Chang, the ice cream maker.

"Neither do I," said Gari, the albino Russian musician.

"Then the bass must be safe and healthy," I said. "Good." I turned and fixed my gaze on the parking lot attendant. "I'm drawn to that man," I said. "Let's regard him from here. He's not young, as you see, but he goes about his work with a youthful air, moving sprightly among his cars."

We were about nine cars away, and Charlie Pino said, "If you like him, Don Pippo, why don't we go right up to him?"

Every morning of every season, I explained, I contemplated asking that attendant whether he knew at what point the fresh water turns to salt. But in the end I decided not to burden him with a difficult question from, as far as he knew, an ordinary runner and then, in my old age, an ordinary walker. I did not wish to distract him from his diligent work of guiding cars to vacant spots and ticketing and making sure all the cars were parked straight as soldiers. Most of all, I did not wish to give him the opportunity of departing from the good cheer he showed me when I passed. I'd call out to him from afar, "And how are you this morning, my good man?"

He'd find me and tip his baseball cap and smile.

I saluted him going and coming, and did not pass on until he tipped his cap and smiled. One morning I succumbed to the temptation of learning his name.

"Jerry!" he called out.

"And where do you live, Jerry?"

"New Jersey," he returned.

Now I looked with infinite pleasure across the river to New Jersey. I was comfortable not desiring to know exactly where in New Jersey Jerry lived. Such a lovely man, certainly a happy family man, lived everywhere in New Jersey. Thus I resolved that there are at least two types of ignorance: intentional ignorance, from which I suffer, pray for me, Jerry! and pure ignorance. Jerry will ascend to Dante with the goodness he showed me preserved in his heart, purely ignorant of the knowledge that throughout all the days he worked his lot, I owned it, and the men and women he guided in and out may have appeared like teachers at that college across the highway or like businessmen of Wall Street, but they were my soldiers. And, at night, when Jerry was warm with his family in their mobile home in Jersey beside a peaceful wood, trucks marked *Wholesale Fish* came here and among the fish were the bodies of my enemies. They were unloaded into that dumpster there and then up, up, up and over into the river. The water below us appears stagnant and foul, but I know the tides. I know them from observing the piers that used to jut into the river busted up. Ungathered wood lingers here a while, then drifts out to the ocean.

Come September

"On second thought, Johnny, down in the Bahamas let's not bring up the odious manner in which the kid professor talks about his wife. I'll take care of it later on. He's been blabbering about inviting me to his university for a reading, and I believe he will because he wants to use my work in his Ph.D. thesis on ethnic literature and needs my permission. I'm the subject of his chapter on the avant garde. So I'll fly to Philadelphia, read my heart out, then I'll collar him and take him to a café. Vivid in his memory will be the writing he so ardently admires, it will be a moment of profound trust and faith, and then I'll say in the guttural tone of a paesano, 'Ted, how exactly do you feel about your wife?' The truth will emerge, I'm certain, and then once we have it, we can prescribe the appropriate public posture. What do you say?"

"Just touch on his wife down in the Bahamas? I see, you want to plant the seed, in literature it's called simply a *plant*, an idea or character established and then seemingly abandoned, the reader believes it has gone forever, but sometimes this idea or that character reappears and figures in a big way and the reader finds that it had etched itself in the memory and delights in the cohesiveness of it all. You believe that the kid professor's innermost feelings about his wife are interrelated with his imaginary life of crime, and I agree wholeheartedly, and so you wish to intimate that his wife's life will be in jeopardy if he doesn't shut up about the crime now. But don't you think, Johnny, that fear for his wife's life will register immediately, powerfully, right there on the veranda, and he will go to pieces, fear losing its efficacy as a device? I think so. The sad truth is that, like love, only so much fear can be held at any given moment. Believe me,

Johnny, I've tried, in every moment of my life I've tried to embrace all the past images and protestations of love, from the warm, viscous security of my mother's womb to the incessant effusions of love for my girlfriend. Now, after fifty years, each moment explodes like a Samex bomb concealed in a radio in the baggage compartment. I and my images bust up and go flying into thin air. I grasp for the future. Am reduced to whimpering about it.

"Just the other afternoon, Lefty was sprawled naked in my single bed. I leaned down slowly and kissed her belly. It was smooth and flat and looked hard, but went warm and soft with the kiss. Then I felt compelled to interrupt the sweet reverie. 'For the first time in my life, I have a plan,' I said. 'Come September, we will go to Key West and live together.' She had expressed the desire to visit Hemingway's house. 'We will visit Hemingway's house,' I couldn't restrain myself from continuing, 'and then find rooms of our own overlooking the Gulf, and every early evening we will walk along the beach's promenade into the sunset.'

"'I have to go,' she quipped.

"I reached out for her but she brushed aside my hands, those same hands, Johnny, about which she sighs: 'Your hands, your hands, I love your hands on me.' She slipped on her black leather skirt and black, lace fringed bra, then darted into the bathroom. On summer days around six o'clock, when she was leaving, the sun was low on the horizon and shined onto her hair. A *castagna*, it was the color of a chestnut, that warm, satisfying delicacy we have after our holiday feasts. Her lipstick which Bendel's mixed specially for her matched her hair, and while she applied a fresh layer to her full, puckered lips, I stared at her reflection from a corner of the bedroom. The skin of her face was taut, clear, but on the side that I could see, I saw a line of pain, it tugged at her youthful beauty from her hairline to the bottom of her jaw. The kind of deep pain that had surfaced on my father's face as he struggled to take a few steps with his walker. I sat down in his old yellow armchair.

"I heard the newspaper fall. I had bought *The New York Times* because she told me it was for everybody. I didn't know where to put it, and left it teetering on top of the wicker hamper. The back of one of her legs had knocked the paper down. She picked it up. Knocked it down again. I heard her begin to breathe heavily, then I heard the click of her heels on the marble tiles, then on the kitchen linoleum.

"'I can't take this,' her words preceded her.

"'Take what?' I said.

"She was within view now, putting on her leather

motorcycle jacket. 'Every afternoon you bring up the future. You refuse to see what we have now.' Then she screamed, 'I'm here! I'm here!' Her voice was raspy now, which I love, it's a sound of love, and with it she uttered the most frightening words men such as ourselves can hear. 'I think we shouldn't see each other for a while.'

"'A while?' I repeated in an attempt to erase the idea.

"'A few days,' she said forlornly, which, of course, I took to mean forever.

"'Don't go,' I croaked. 'Please don't go.' She sat in a straight chair, and then I said, 'I'll never mention the future again.'"

The Word

Tears come to my eyes for no apparent reason, at least no reason apparent to my nurse, Italia. She dries my tears, then the beads of sweat on my brow, on my neck. She cups my chin tenderly. "What's wrong, Don Pippo?" she humors me.

"Nothing, nothing..."

"Are you contemplating dying again?"

"Of course. I contemplate dying every day. Everybody should contemplate dying every day. Especially we Italians. That's one of our troubles, we have no respect for death. It could be the weather."

"But you said you'll live as long as you can use your...your..."

"Say it, Italia, say *prick*! I said I'll live as long as I can use my prick to fuck my wife, she needs it. Why can't you use the precise word to describe what you have in mind and in heart. It's understandable, I guess.

"From the beginning, words confused us. Do you know what Italian kids of my generation grew up thinking duty was? Huh? Shit! That's right, shit! When our parents saw that we had to go, when they saw that look of alarm come over our faces and the bowl was a relatively new idea, they'd say: 'Go do your duty.' Plop! Duty! Plop shit! 'How wonderful, I'm doing my duty,' we'd say to ourselves. And we don't know where our asshole is, because if we had trouble going, we were told to pound our knees with our fists. Shit duty resided in our kneecaps. The more trouble we had going, the harder we pounded, reddening our knees, our hands. And so shit duty involved pain: shit duty pain. No wonder we're all anal retentive. Anyway, I'm not married, so how can I use my…"

"There's always the future..."

"We have no future. Our only future is intermarriage."

"I meant, Don Pippo," Italia chokes, "are you contemplating killing yourself?"

"Except for a few pieces of minor business, my work is done, and as a gift to myself I wish to die and I wish to die in the old fashioned way, by assassination. But I must not know the means or the identities of my assassins so that I can derive pleasure from contemplating them. All the rest is crystal clear. The site is here, in the shrine. And once I'm dead, my body is hacked into parts with the long knife my grandfather fashioned with his hands in his deep, dark cellar. And then my parts are placed in medium size plastic trash bags which my assassins throw over their shoulders and carry down the stairs, and then out they go into the dark of night toward the river. The bags are dumped in the dumpster in the parking lot located where the fresh water turns to salt, and then up, up and over into the river.

"My tears are tears of joy because I see my parts linger a while in the still and stagnant water. My head rises to the surface and bobs, and the face is that of a young Don Pippo, handsome, sublime; his beautiful hazel eyes open to the immensity of the sky; and the brothers and sisters on the embankment marvel at the curled lashes the way the old ladies under the el used to marvel at them. My black hat is on, nail it on if need be, and around my head like a nimbus, the fingers splayed, float my beautiful hands. So let out the word, sweet Italia, and seal my desire with a kiss."

The L Word

Early in our fascination Lefty says, "Usually when I start up with somebody I know how long it'll last. 'Three, four months max,' I say to myself, but with you it's different, with you I can't see the end."

"The end will come when I die," I tell her and then later on concoct the scene, the death scene.

I'm in the kitchen cooking of a Saturday night and she's in the dining room-bedroom, sitting in the yellow club chair. "I love you," I pronounce from the stove. Midway through my life, I find myself professing love to Lefty over and over, so much so that it's like professing it for the two of us, which she senses this Saturday night.

She gets up and stands at the threshold of the two rooms. I turn and look at her. She says, "The words come hard for me. The word *love* is the biggest lie in the English language. But I'm crazy about you."

"If it will make you feel more comfortable," I say, "use the Yiddish form, the Italian form. *Libe. Amore.*"

She chuckles, but then later on, naked in bed which I'm passing on my way to the kitchen again, she says, "Would you feel better if I used the L word?" Instead of replying, "If you so desire," I say, "That's all right."

After we make love again, the hour tolling eleven, the hour of her departure, I tell her, "I'm about to die and I'm alone, but in the final moment I see you sitting at the edge of the bed, on the beige quilt stained with your blood. You're calm, prim, serious. I fix a last ghastly look on your fresh, young face and manage a smile, and with my last breath croak, 'Please say you love me.' You remain silent, straight-faced, true to your belief to the end. Still smiling, I turn my face to the wall and die."

A few days later Lefty calls and says, "Can I have your permission to use the death scene in my novel?"

The scene resurrects itself and I feel all of my youthful love for her and ageless sorrow. At the same time, I understand her struggle as a young writer. "Yes," I say, "you can use the scene. But then can I use it myself?"

"No," she says.

A Warm Piece of Bread

I ascend to my shrine through my nurse Italia's fragrance, Ysatis by Givenchy. She's upstairs preparing my breakfast, Pecan Splendor, which she claims is a healthy mixture of   oats, raisins, cinnamon, whey and, of course, pecan nuts,   all sloshing around in a sea of vanilla soy milk. Employing my last ounce of strength, I arrive at my door which I keep open a dagger's width so that from the landing I can see my throne, my yellow chair. I do not want to open my door to the absence of a woman and music and children. Also, I leave open my door in keeping with a tradition set by General Giuseppe Garibaldi, who unhinged his doors and smashed the glass of his windows in reaction to a memory from his childhood in Nice, where a tax was levied according to how many doors and windows you had. But my door,

Don Pippo's door, is closed! My brittle shoulder presses against it, and I break out into a cold sweat and feel faint and close my eyes, where in the infinite darkness I see the frenzied spots of all colors which I saw when I was about to faint in church when I was a boy. "Italia, Italia," I whisper, "it's me, your Don. The war of the five families is over."

"The password!" she cries.

"I say, 'Brother now' and the response is: 'Forever.'"

"I'm sorry, go away!"

"But that *was* our secret code and then we changed it and I forget. Is it, 'Unity and Independence'?"

"Nope!"

"Ysatis by Givenchy?"

"That's my perfume, how do you know it?"

"I'm your Don, he knows everything."

"Prove it"

"Married men are your friends for a while, sometimes as long as two years, and then they become your lovers. You make a point of distinguishing between love and sex; you've had four miscarriages, adopted two kids and now your daughter, after taking up with some foreign guy and then finding out who her biological mother is, won't talk to you."

Italia opens the door, and I collapse into her soft, fair arms. She carries me to my yellow throne then applies compresses of alcohol onto my bald head. "And you went out without your bodyguards," she reprimands me.

"I like to think I'm beyond fear."

"That may be," Italia says, "but you're not beyond danger. Did you at least take your gun?"

"My gun?"

"Yes, your gun."

"The pure in mind and heart," I sigh, "do not need weapons, we need seed and soil. Even the great warrior Garibaldi did not carry a weapon, he picked one up before the battle. In October 1860, after handing Naples and Sicily to King Victor, unifying Italy for the first time since the fall of the Roman Empire, the weary general rejected titles and land grants and a dowry for his daughter, Teresita. The only gift to himself was some coffee purchased with a loan and a sack of seed, corn for his animals. He tossed the sack over his broad shoulders and retired to his island of Caprera. The soil was barren, dry, yet with his hands Garibaldi burrowed and planted. "Where's my dagger?" I ask Italia.

"At least you're thinking of carrying a dagger."

"Please hold the door open with it, from my throne I must see the landing, the iron banister. Rest assured I know who's approaching. I can tell from the weight and slide of the step, the force of the breath, the smell. I knew you were here, Italia, from all the way down by the river. By the way, mind if I give Don Ralph the name of your perfume? He smelled it on you and would like to suggest the brand to his lady."

"I don't want any other woman wearing my perfume, especially Don Ralph's. She's twenty and he's eighty. I think that's disgusting!"

"One moment of pleasure for men our age is worth all the fragrances in the world. Just think, your fragrance stimulating Don Ralph instead of an electric rod."

"Don Pippo, you're disgusting!"

"Yes, and a victim of this so called changing realities. Tell me again, what do you mean by it?"

"Eat the Pecan Splendor."

"All right, but first explain about the changing realities. Funny thing, I forget the explanation and the realities, too."

"Well, one day you say red is your favorite color and the next day you say green."

"Naturally, they're the colors of our flag! Red for the fire of our volcanoes, green for…"

"Please eat your breakfast, Don Pippo. It's seven o'clock and people are coming over with their daily requests."

"What time?"

"You let out the word that you cannot refuse a request between ten p.m. and midnight."

"Did I say that?"

"Yes. You said those are the hours you feel most

lonely."

"Please bring me a cup of coffee and one piece of toast. That's been the traditional Napoli Sicilia breakfast ever since I can remember, every morning at sunrise we gathered around the kitchen table, each of us with a cup of coffee and one piece of toast. My mother and her sisters and their mother turned their gaze out the window toward the el and just beyond to the man who flew pigeons. I beg you, Italia, one piece of toast and a cup of coffee with a drop of ordinary milk and a grain or two of cane sugar."

"The Pecan Splendor is good for you, Don Pippo."

"But I can't chew it," I reply, then open my mouth, revealing one canine.

"You eat steaks with one tooth, you can eat the Pecan Splendor." She brings me a bowl set on an inlaid brass tray I bought my mother in Casablanca.

"Please bring me a fork."

"You eat cereal with a spoon."

"I eat ice cream with a fork, I can eat cereal with one."

Italia hands me a fork and I begin to eat.

"Don Pippo, you went out this morning with the gas on under the frying pan and no gas coming out. I had to open the window and, since you have no air freshener, I sprinkled some perfume."

"Did you feed the sparrows and water the geranium?"

"You see! Yesterday you said that only *you* can feed the sparrows and water the geranium. You said that on her death bed your mother told you to remember to put out a bowl of fresh water for the sparrows."

"I remember. I apologize."

"Why did you turn the gas on under the frying pan?"

"To make myself a piece of toast."

"In a frying pan? fried toast?"

"I'd do anything, Italia, for a warm piece of bread."

An Ordinary Man

"Help me to change, Johnny. Help me to change from a lover to an ordinary man. By lover I don't necessarily mean a big man with the ladies, I mean the way I view everything. For instance, I don't know what my father really felt when he first saw my mother. It's my contention that pity superseded love, that he surrendered the love of his life for a strange woman's fleeting pain, her gash, her fount of blood. When he made love to this injured woman on a night shortly after he consoled her, maybe he had a good time and wanted to repeat that good time every night for the rest of his life. After a few days away from Lily, he may have decided that a Brooklyn boy was out of place in Halifax, in a fishing village surrounded by forests protected by Canadian Mounties. A life with my mother was a way of staying home, which he may have desired even before he traveled north. Now in Brooklyn he foresaw the comfort and security of taking up with a local girl, setting up an office in the old neighborhood and alleviating the toothaches of people he knew, had grown up with.

"From the time I was a boy and from the time I was a man, whenever I looked at him and saw his head turned away, angled at the heavens, it was my idea that the image before his glazed eyes was that of the fair, beautiful Lily. He probably had a thousand other images before his eyes. Beginning with the fetus growing inside Gertie's belly. He spent four tortuous months picturing it before deciding to marry the mother. He married her in Our Lady of Guadalupe church. Had a huge brick house built just around the corner from his childhood home and two blocks away from his wife's home, on the other side of the el, the side closer to the ocean. He set up a modern office in the basement and worked six days a week from nine to nine. In short, Johnny, he became an ordinary man, and the apple isn't supposed to fall far from the tree, right? I want to become an ordinary man, too. Please help me."

Johnny rubs his narrow, pointy chin. A boyish chin supporting a man's face, a serious man's face. He gets up abruptly and paces to and from the buffet table.

"It's hopeless, isn't it, Johnny? You might as well take out your gun and shoot me now."

"Too easy. Shhh," and he continues to pace, to think. Finally, his words drift back to me.

Johnny grants that my autobiography is my autobiography. Even if I didn't witness any of its events, if that's how I see it, that's how it is. This is a fact, Johnny says, and no one, even he, can dispute it. But, Johnny addends, if I could be more specific, lend some detail to the locales, say, all for the purpose of making them concrete, then I'd be convinced of the truth of the images and they'll stop haunting me and I'll be able to view life in all of its complexities, not just through a kaleidoscope of love. "You know how we say," Johnny concludes, smiling with satisfaction. *"Passa tutto.* Everything passes."

"I'll try, Johnny," I tell him. "I'll try real hard."

Though thousands of miles separate the three central images, they resurrect immediately and I feel comfortable with all they contain and inspire. I'm about to tell Johnny the good news when the locales begin to move. They gather momentum, tremendous force and speed. But then they stop abruptly at the threshold of a new locale. The place where I was conceived, I sense, but I can't see it. There are two parts, an inner part and an outer part. The inner part is

209

my mother's vaginal canal, it grows clear, but the outer part remains in darkness.

"Johnny," I say, "the three locales pose no problem. But a fourth locale has arisen. Would you like to hear about it?"

"Yes," Johnny says, "but in time. Please start at the beginning."

I've never been to Halifax and so have not passed through its Southeast Railway Station, where Lily and Willie say their final farewell and where Lily sits on a bench on the platform and waits fifty one years. I juxtapose to Halifax a station I in fact know, the Milan station, where I waited one late cold night for a train to Bologna. A great convex, translucent dome covered this station, making it eternally gray, damp. I carry the dome on my imagination's shoulders over the Alps, over Western Europe, over the Straits of

Gibraltar and then across the Atlantic, taking the northern route to Nova Scotia.

Halifax, I discover, was the chief naval station of British North America and the terminus of a host of railroads: the Canadian Pacific, International, Southwestern, as well as the Southeastern. And so in the eternal season of gray dampness there's an incessant coming and going of sailors falling in and out of their sweethearts' arms. Two lovers stand close together, whispering a vow of eternal love; she in a red coat, he in a blue cashmere suit.

Willie's bedroom in Brooklyn where he packs his things became a shrine to an Italian boy out in the world. I passed the room a thousand times on my way from my grandmother's bedroom to the kitchen. Always peeked in and saw that it was a small room with one window kept closed even in the summertime. The air was stale, danced with dust. The straight chair around which Willie hangs his jacket stood against a wall, in a corner beside a bureau. The bed on which he packs his suitcase was made with the same white cotton coverlet.

One locale edited out of the original autobiography is the lay of the land between Willie's house and Slim's. The way is irregular because the avenue before Slim's house curves ever so slightly, following the el overhead. The dark, bending avenue tosses a vacant lot here, a gas station there, a garden of weeds, wild flowers. The West End line begins in Coney Island, where Willie liked to go, to amusement parks. The train rises and rounds serpentine like out of the southern horizon toward Bensonhurst, stays out in the open until the tunnel under the East River. The line ends in the heart of New York, where Willie also liked to go, Vesuvio's, Radio City. The entire course from Coney Island to New

York assumes the shape of a wide, subtle boomerang. Willie stops deep in the shadows. He looks left, right. Checks his Hamilton watch, 7:15. Slim, waiting on the corner, calls him.

The third locale, Slim's dining room where Willie sits for fifty one years, I sat at that table every Sunday afternoon at the left of my grandfather. He faced the windows draped with linen curtains. The crystal chandelier illuminated my terror, his veiny, mushroom nose, dead beady eyes close together, the fastidious way he carved the head of fish and ate them.

"Which brings us, Johnny, to the new locale, the fourth. I see my mother's vaginal canal. It's long, luminous, viscous, resilient. I see the fateful sperm burrowing, swimming along with millions of others. I see the explosion. But where are they, Johnny? I want to know where my mother and father are. Where he has taken her, where she has taken him. The Red Devils' clubhouse? Somewhere around Wall Street? What room, Johnny? What room in what place?"

The Clown and the Lamppost

Seeing my tears, Italia begins to cry. She approaches and sprawls her eel like body across my meager lap and beyond the arms of the yellow throne covered with my mother's linen napkins fringed with lace. Then, as if out of nowhere, I feel the warmth and softness of a kiss.

"You mustn't go, Don Pippo. The hallway is packed with problems only you can solve, the line goes down to the street, up the block and around the corner, the way the line used to be when your father took you to Radio City Music Hall. Try to remember your teaching that, when faced with a long, arduous task, we should try to invoke a pleasant scene from childhood, a consoling face, a beautiful song..."

"Give me a moment," I say, and close my eyes. Fresh tears escape them.

"Why are you crying now, Don Pippo?"

"I remember the great love of my life, what was her name?"

"Tina, Catherine, Lydia, Susan, Vita Rose, Susan..."

"I remember telling her that I saw an act, my very first, and I was surrounded by six thousand brothers and sisters. Far, far down in the deep left corner a man played his organ, and his sounds rose and filled the great dark theater. The full orchestra ascended, tuning, playing discordant notes, music stands lit by specks of light. The gold curtain opened onto a street, an empty street at first, but a cozy one because it was the only street in the whole world. A place for all of us to be on, to meet and talk. It was night and the street was dark, except for the bright light of one streetlamp.

"Here comes a clown, a sad looking clown, but when he enters the light of the streetlamp, he smiles and looks around. He gets an idea, a strange, wonderful, dangerous idea, which is to climb the lamppost. He shimmies up to the top and sits there, locks his legs around the lamp, then looks up and down the street. He smiles, and then of all things he begins to rock and the lamppost goes with him, a little to the left, up, a little to the right. He's going to fall off but the clown keeps rocking, rocking harder, and the post whips faster and faster, left, up, right, until it is parallel to the street. He's going to hit the street, but his faithful post takes him up and over to the other side. His arc now is wide, reaching low, as in an embrace of all of us standing in the light on the street."

The Dante Society of Westchester

The nurse Italia is a composite character drawn partially from a woman of our generation from the old neighborhood named Ruby, and so when Sister Ruby came out in a skimpy silk thing and sat cross-legged beside me on her couch, I paid it no mind. She'd send me to the Natural Food Store on Prince Street for her Pecan Splendor, and in return made me gourmet pasta. She lived up by Grand Central Terminal and parked her car in the rooftop garage, in a quiet, dark corner, on top of all those arriving and departing trains. She felt there was time for one last great passion of her life, she told me, and then took up with a married French pilot who made occasional runs to New York.

Ruby was born and raised on our side of the el about where it begins its turn toward Coney Island, toward the ocean. On a quiet, narrow block in God's Country of Bensonhurst, her father slapped her around, and so little Ruby had to watch his every movement around the room. Now when we walked down a street, she squeezed my arm for fear that a hundred feet ahead there was an abyss in the sidewalk.

The hospitable, hard working Italian father dies, and soon Ruby notices another man around the house, Charlie Lucky's brother, who was in the garment business.

One school day around 3:30, he notices Ruby crying. "The boys on the block bother me on my way home from school," she tells him. He picks up the phone. Ruby is on his lap, four feet from the receiver, can see his lips moving but cannot hear a word.

The next day, around 3:30, she turns briskly into her block, books clasped against her chest. All the boys put down their bats and balls and march to the other side of the street and face the buildings and stay there until Ruby is inside. Her elder sister also abused her and at the same time loved Renata Tebaldi's voice, had all her records. And then this sister died, and Ruby kept her record collection and grew to love the opera in general. She made me tapes of Renata Tebaldi singing with the Swedish tenor Jussi Bjorling. In her middle age, long divorced, adopted children making their way, Ruby wanted to write stories and in return for lessons sent Garibaldi to America's philanthropic founding families, the Guggenheims, Mellons, Rockefellers, and God knows where.

"She didn't send your stories, Johnny, preferring to listen to them."

One day Ruby said, "But what happens?"

"The War of the Five Families is over, Ruby," I told

her. "Johnny's trial and all that surrounded it was a charade, made for TV and the papers. Even Anthony Quinn and Mickey Rourke interviewed outside a courthouse was a stroke of genius on Johnny's part, actors playing out a supposed real scene."

"But the sentence...?"

"The last time I saw Johnny he had his Machiavelli with him, and he and Vinny were on their way to a plastic surgeon in Garden City who was going to transform them into blondes with big tits. Then Vinny was going to Vegas, and Johnny to New Orleans."

About a year after Ruby's fund raising efforts, a woman's gravelly voice over the telephone, "Is this Mr...?"

I paused, looked around the room, the shrine. The majority of that person was with Garibaldi in Rio de Janeiro where for the past three days, opposite the fish market, in plain view of the port officials, twelve of us, including Luigi Carniglia and Edoardo Mutru who would die in a shipwreck, have been outfitting our 120 ton ship, the *Mazzini*, for war, hiding a few pieces of old iron and some ammo under meat cured with manioc flour. The enemy is the Empire of Brazil, which has 67 warships carrying 2,830 men, one steamship, 350 guns.

"I was the first woman elected into a society of men, the Dante Society of Westchester--"

We cast the *Mazzini* off from her moorings, enter the causeway...

"Now as events coordinator, I want to break the ice of boat rides, picnics, bingo games."

"Her voice, Johnny, was steeped in suffering and longing, like our mothers', our aunts'."

"You know," the Voice said, "I've gone through a lot of trouble locating you! Your number is unlisted, but I found a book of yours and called the publisher, Lawrence Auerbach, something like that."

"I called him Don Lorenzo. He loved the opera and was fond of recalling something I had told him about the great voices like Caruso, Callas, even Richard Tucker, that they died young because they sang their hearts out."

"We would like you to give a lecture. Money is no problem. Instead of buying a thoroughbred or two that day, the men will pay you."

"Don Lorenzo used to say that he was the only white man Amiri Baraka would talk to. I haven't gotten Amiri's take on this, and Don Lorenzo developed Judith Rossner, got Bill Buckley to writing fiction, but then went bankrupt. I bought up the remainders of my book from the bankruptcy court. 'It's so hard,' his wife told me walking down an east side street. 'I don't want to be a young widow.' They managed to hold on to the phone in his mother's house in East Hampton, that's how you hooked up with me."

"I'm delighted," the Voice said, "that our paths have finally crossed. So many of us do not meet until we have crossed the bridge, leaving behind our roots, our first families, sometimes our first marriages."

"My first friend, Tommy, and I met again after forty years. He'd fallen in love with a Jewish woman who lived in Manhattan the year round. 'I'm afraid of crossing the bridge,' Tommy told me. He married, moved to Manhattan, got a stroke but is playing golf again and looks just fine."

Doris Carubba was her name and she was crying. "I am a widow. My husband died earlier this year, in January. I loved my husband. Now I have my grown kids, work."

"I heard about this Italian fellow out in California who only has to hear the word 'pizza' and he breaks down. He should walk into any pizzeria around the country and look at the name on the ovens, or go and see *Do the Right Thing* and look behind Sal the Pizza Man at the name on his oven. *Bari,* it says, and for an interesting afternoon the Californian and Spike Lee could go down to the Bowery between Houston and Prince and ask around for this Bari, say Nicholas sent them, and a five by five man would appear with a face the shape of a full moon, pants he hitches over his belly. Ask him about America's first fast food, pizza, and Bari will tell them how mass production was made possible by his father manufacturing the first pizza oven down there, and invented the cheese grater, and then in trucks his ovens and graters made their way over the highways and byways, to all corners. I must tell you," I went on, she was chuckling now, "at a funeral recently in Brooklyn, under the el, the men went out back for a smoke, on a stairwell overlooking the rear parking lot, and out of nowhere Bari slapped my cheek and said: 'See this guy, he's the only one who never stole from me.'"

"The lecture is December 9th."

"I'll talk a little on Garibaldi."

"You don't understand. We want a lecture on Dante!"

"On Dante! But you people…"

"Are you kiddin? I'm president of Estelle Wedding Gowns, Ltd., and I'll send you our current year book, you'll see who we are. I have blonde hair."

"And I'll be wearing a black hat."

"Rocco's of Westchester. I'll send a limo."

I remembered telling Lefty over the phone that if I had known at the function that she was married, I wouldn't have gone out with her.

"Really," she had said.

I repeated, "If I had known…"

"Do you think that would have stopped Dante, if Beatrice was married."

"They were nine years old when they met," I said. "Dante's father had taken him along to her father's house, and Dante saw her for the first time walking down a staircase. 'Her dress on that day was of a most noble color, a subdued and goodly crimson, girdled and adorned in such sort as best suited with her tender age. At that moment I saw most truly that the spirit of life which hath its dwelling place in the secret chamber of the heart began to tremble so violently that the least pulses of my body shook therewith, and in trembling it said these words, "Lo, a god mightier than I who comes to have dominion over me."""

Doris Carubba called often throughout the summer, the fall, and on weekends from her car phone on her way to her country house in Montauk where she had a horse, Rosa, a chestnut filly with a disease that began in the bloodstream then spread to the bone, but with lots of care and oats and carrots, Rosa survived the summer. The gravel of Doris' voice mingled with the sounds of night traffic, roars of tons of steel through air. "The annual ball is coming up and my brother in law said he'd go with me. I don't want to go alone and I'm afraid of being seen with another man. I'm supposed to give out the scholarships."

"Go alone," I advised, which she did, and left early, after the scholarships, and was delighted.

"Ya know, Pietro Di Donato lives out by me...."

"Pete sent an excerpt of his new book, *American Gospels*, with a note to a kid professor friend of mine. The note read, 'I'd rather have a *paisano* who isn't an agent than an agent who isn't a *paisano*.'"

"The Portuguese greengrocer down my block harasses me..."

"Do this," I told her. "The next time you're checking out your items, tell him very quietly, with a smile, that you have a cousin and his name is Johnny, and Johnny wants to hear all about what's going on."

"You know, Johnny, she did this, she told the Portuguese greengrocer she has a cousin named Johnny and the guy stopped and now she goes shopping in peace."

It had snowed earlier in the day, a light dusting, the highway was clear, and I asked the driver to let me off a few blocks away. I wanted to take a solitary walk, savor the moments before meeting Doris Carubba, feel the weight of two dozen copies of my book in my red satchel.

"It's freezing out," the driver said. "Besides, where we're going there are no sidewalks."

He left me off on the sleeve. As Rocco's main entrance was in the rear, I was able to walk a while, skirt perennial manicured lawns, trimmed hedges, tall pines decorated with snow. Rocco's parking lot was also in the rear. Drivers at the wheel, caps on, windows up, motors running.

I wandered inside the banquet hall, spun in and out of huge, crowded rooms, God knows what sacramental occasions. "I have blonde hair," Doris had told me, "and I'll be wearing a black hat." In the middle of one room, someone jumped me. The black Stetson went flying, tinted glasses knocked askew. She cupped my face and kissed it, brief, hard, then stepped back, and we smiled. "The Florida chapter has come up for an emergency meeting, so you only have a few minutes. You're on first."

She ushered me into the banquet room, the heart of it an enormous parquet dance floor, surrounded on two sides with long dining tables. At the far, windowless end, lectern and mike looked onto the dance floor, and beyond to an endless buffet table. Fires under the chafing dishes, platters of antipasto, cold cuts, breads, enough for the One Thousand. Doris ordered the waiters to bring in more. In no time waiters in white jackets marched back in in procession, platters aloft.

She had set up a book table with a white linen cloth. I sat nearby at an ordinary table and watched her in motion, waited. One member with a Florida tan, silver hair, insurance salesman, he would tell me, ambled over and leafed through a book, settling on the Contents page. There's a portrait of Joe D. "Hey, I played golf with Joe yesterday!" and the salesman turned and came over.

"How's Joe?" looking up.

"He's coming along just fine after the heart surgery. How much, the book?"

"Fifteen dollars." Hardcover, 20% discount.

"Fifteen dollars?" he repeated.

"Too much?"

"No, but then you need five dollars' change and nobody here..." and he gestured around the hall "nobody here carries five dollars." He handed me a twenty and then went from one member to another, tapping on shoulders, holding out his right hand. "Give me twenty dollars," I read his lips, then he'd nod at the book. He returned to my table and, like a miracle, a host of twenty dollar bills floated down.

The member chosen to introduce me was a high school principal in hot water with the society for showing sex education films. I adjusted the mike and sought to incorporate the men into the vision before my eyes, the dance floor, by directing my voice and my eyes all around.

"Brothers and Sisters" a few of the wives had come along "Brothers and Sisters, I'd like to donate my Dante to the Society," and held the journey aloft, like a torch. The President came up and accepted, beaming, nodding. "Brothers and Sisters was the form of address used by members of our first revolutionary underground society with political purposes, *Young Italy*, conceived by Giuseppe Mazzini in a prison cell in Savona..."

Two hundred dark suits rustled, the first fork tinkled, bounced onto the dance floor....

"I have time only to make a plea, that you read the book. Please do not feel incapable of understanding it. Dante wrote it in the vulgar tongue, da vernacular, they call it, so that housewives could understand it..."

A glass hit the floor and exploded...

"We are the stuff Dante wrote about, and Dante is the stuff of us. In fact, we *are* Dante and Dante is *us*. I realized this while walking down Bleecker Street one day and a wealthy friend of mine asked: 'Where can I get a gourmet dish of pasta?'"

"At Rocco's!" the men shouted in unison, laughing.

"I suddenly grew sad and didn't know why. Contemplated giving him the name of restaurants supplied by fresh pasta makers, contemplated making him a dish myself, but was still dissatisfied and sad. I was unable to tell him what I truly thought, that our friendship amounted to a gourmet dish of pasta because for him I *was* pasta, in just the same way each one of us *is* Dante. Dante is the Father of Italy," I went on, "Garibaldi is the Father of Modern Italy. I've been wondering, who is the Mother of Italy?"

Entire set ups, glasses, plates...

"Mazzini: 'Love and respect woman. Look to her not only for comfort, but for strength and inspiration and the doubling of your intellectual powers...'"

Music came on...

"I guess it's time for dancing, fellas! Garibaldi!: 'A woman is a divinity to whom one never appeals in vain, when the appeal is from the heart and, above all, when one is beset by misfortune...'"

The mike went dead...

"Closing with a few words about the first Italian patriot, Silvio Pellico, a frail magazine editor arrested and imprisoned by Austria for his magazine and for being seen talking to a revolutionary in a boat on the Po.

"Pellico's dungeon was in a prison in Venice; it overlooked a courtyard, and beyond the court he could see the top of St. Mark's, the pigeons who flew up there from the square and perched on the minarets. Pellico tried to get through at first with thoughts of his family, their last meeting. His father had accompanied him about a mile on his way, and Pellico turned and turned again, kissing the ring his mother had given him. In his dungeon he pricked his finger with the pin he had and with his blood scribbled, 'the Bible and my Dante are getting me through.' Each day he committed a canto to memory. He got through also by praying, praying without cease, 'permitting no one thought which should not be inspired by a wish to conform my whole life to the desires of God.' Pellico grew more cheerful, even sang and whistled. He made a friend, a deaf and dumb boy, five or six, an orphan, child of robbers. Little Deaf and Dumb used to come under his window and smile. Pellico threw him a piece of bread, and the boy took it, leapt for joy, ran to his companions and divided it, and returned to eat his own share under the window.

"'He seemed always happy, lighthearted as the son of a grandee. From him I learned that the mind need not depend on situation. Govern the imagination and we shall be well, wherever we happen to be placed. A day is soon over and, if at night we can retire to rest without actual pain and hunger, it matters little whether it be within the walls of a prison or in the kind of building they call a palace.'

"Pellico was taken through a large vault that led to another courtyard, where the female prisoners were kept with those laboring with disease. A single, thin wall separated him from some of the women. He listened to their song, late at night heard them talk. One voice was so very sweet that it grew dear to him. Her name was Maddalene. He heard her sighs of consolation: 'Courage, courage, my poor dears...' She sang little, mostly kept repeating, 'Ah, who will give the lost one her vanished dream of bliss? Ah, who will give the lost one her vanished dream of bliss?' Pellico: 'Woman is for me a creature so admirable, so sublime, the mere seeing, hearing and speaking to her enriches my mind with such...'"

AV 2013

Anthony Valerio is the author of several books of fiction & non-fiction. His work has been collected in anthologies & readers. Mr. Valerio has taught at NYU, the City University of New York & Wesleyan University. He is a member of the Author's Guild & PEN.